THE
GERMAN
DOCTOR'

THE
GERMAN
DOCTOR

LUCÍA PUENZO

TRANSLATED BY
DAVID WILLIAM FOSTER

nova

Published by Hesperus Nova
Hesperus Press Limited
28 Mortimer Street, London W1W 7RD
www.hesperuspress.com

This edition first published by Hesperus Press Limited, 2014

Designed and typeset by Roland Codd

Printed in the United States of America

ISBN: 978-1-84391-543-0

PART ONE
HERLITZKA

1

That day, a mixture of sodium chloride and magnesium nitrate, injected with infinite patience into each eyeball, would change forever the course of science. The mass sterilisations, the vivisections, the frustrated attempts to change skin and hair colour using subcutaneous injections and even the night on which he thought he had finally succeeded in joining together the veins of two twins to create Siamese twins, only to find them a few hours later gasping like fish out of water – all his failures would be forgotten if he could manage to change the colour of the eyes of this child. He had imagined at least a thousand times holding the only surviving Romanian twin whose left iris had been coloured by the dye (albeit after an overdose had burned his right one), standing on the stage of every medical Racial Hygiene congress in which he had participated during the last decade. The boy's optical nerves paralysed by an excess of chemicals and his pupils dilated with terror, in the arms of the person who had jabbed him something like a thousand times until he had finally freed him from mediocrity. He had dreamed of him with his head shaved to allow the black fuzz of his origins to be eclipsed by a future Aryan. Although he understood it was only a dream, the images of that first life in which everything was possible were obliterated by the certainty that his victory was only the harbinger of all the transformations that were to come (including moulding genetically the citizens of an entire nation), even if up until then had only been lacerated skin, gangrene and amputations. Their investment of millions of Deutschmarks had not been in vain. All in the name of the purity of blood and genes. That was the real war: purity vs contamination.

He sat down on the bed with the excitement of a child preparing for a day at the amusement park. Only then did the surroundings of his rented room with its sparse decor return him to the shaky present. It was all a mirage. Every day his skin hung looser and his ruined muscle tone was that of an old man. His entire existence had turned grey, days and nights of identical routine repeated ad nauseam, in the secret hope something would happen. Someone was going to inform him they had finally stopped searching for him, or they had arranged the journey across the border to his next stop. He had devoted his life to freeing the world of rats and now, on the run and a coward, banished to the shadows and the fringes of the world, he had turned into a fleeing rat himself.

Life cannot reduce itself to just this, he thought.

When he received the warning that they were on his trail, he didn't doubt it was true for a moment: he froze the samples of bacteriology in terminal specimens he had been working on in recent months, walked out of his laboratory, stopped at the bank to empty his account, and drove until he left the city behind. He was never going to lack money: his bottomless family fortune had been supplemented by the contributions of his mentor, Professor von Verschuer, who worked at the Kaiser-Wilhelm-Institut in Dahlem and who had always taken it upon himself to obtain the necessary underwriting for his work in exchange for being the first to receive the results of his experiments. Even in Mengele's exile, von Verschuer was one of the many who continued to contribute anonymously to this well-being, convinced that it was only a matter of time before he could resume his studies. There were many who

8

continued to believe in him, supporting him from a distance, from the shadows, and writing him long letters in which they treated him like a mentor. An illustrious man. Theirs were not excessive words of praise, but the acknowledgement that gave him the strength to go on.

He bought supplies at a petrol station and a map of Argentina before calling his wife. He didn't tell her where he was headed. He told her he would be gone for a time and asked her to stay for a few weeks with a couple of friends, hanging up before she could protest. He drove for ten hours before stopping at a roadside motel on the outskirts of Chacharramendi. In reality the town didn't really have a downtown or outskirts, since it ended in the same block where it began. He stayed in the room until it grew dark. Although his Spanish was fluent, he took out his dictionary and the notebook in which he wrote out his daily correspondence class. Like all survivors, he knew he had to erase some tracks as soon as possible. His mind was more a soldier's than a scientist's, and his first training had been the moulding that comes from the blows of military discipline received in the ranks. He never let a day go by without doing his written and oral exercises.

'I'm a pharmacist,' he repeated three times, making an effort to improve his pronunciation. 'My favourite activity is lis… tening to opera with my son.'

He lied, used to protecting himself even when he was alone. He couldn't even remember his first-born's features. In the only photograph he'd kept, his son was babbling his first words, mindless to the butchery to which his father had dedicated his existence.

A little girl's cry startled him as he was about to answer the next question out loud. He pulled a yellowing curtain aside and saw a group of little girls playing in the car park.

9

Two of them were turning a skipping rope in circles, faster and faster, while singing as fast as they could something that sounded like a mantra, given the hypnotic devotion with which they repeated a monotonous verse. They were dark-skinned, children of a mixed race, except for one… She would have made a perfect specimen (blonde, fair-skinned, with clear eyes) if it hadn't been for her height. Visibly small for her age, although with arms and legs normal enough, the child who jumped faster and faster before his eyes could be an example that defined one of his favourite fields of study: dwarfism, taken to be the exemplary category of the abnormal. She had managed to absorb some Aryan genes, but not enough to lose her animal features. These were the lab rats that most fascinated him: perfect except for one intolerable defect.

When her challenger gave up, she cried out for more. To his surprise, her voice did not match her deformity. It was an octave lower than what he would have expected. She didn't seem afraid of the rope hitting her on her head or heels.

She didn't seem afraid of anything.

That evening he saw her sitting on the pavement with three of the dark-skinned girls, playing jacks. She was the one to toss in the air the tiny sacks of rice grains, trapping them with the same hand that held one more jack. He was whistling Tosca's final aria, *Addio alla vita*, when he stopped to observe her. Her motor skills and her reflexes were excellent, above average. Each one of her movements was an apex of vitality. It was obvious. The dark-skinned girls were locals and the blonde wasn't from around there, a circus professional who had them captivated by some unknown game.

'Time for dinner, Lilith!'

'I'm not hungry!'

'I didn't ask you if you were hungry! I told you to come and have your dinner!'

The boy who was shouting was standing in the doorway of the motel, an adolescent about sixteen years old, as blonde and fit as she was and delightfully arrogant. There was no doubting they were brother and sister, although the measurements of the small South American Adonis were perfect. He would have given anything at that moment to know their parents and grandparents so he could delve into the family tree to understand at what fork in the road the one guilty of degrading the race was to be found.

'Is everything all right, sir?'

He turned and saw the motel owner watching him as he smoked a cigar on the veranda. Except for the blonde children, the rest of the town seemed to move in slow motion, rendered lethargic by the flatness of the desert. That afternoon he'd counted on the fingers of one hand the inhabitants who had dragged their chairs out to the pavement to drink a couple of *matés* before the darkness forced them to take refuge in their caves.

'There's an inn nearby if you'd like something to eat.'

'Where?'

'Two blocks straight ahead… You can't miss it.'

'Is it likely to be open?'

'It always is.'

Out of the corner of his eye he saw that the little girl was walking toward the boy, swaying her hips as she tossed in the air one of the little sacks of rice and caught it with her hand. She moved with the grace of a ballerina, unaware of her limitations. There was something enchanting about her boldness. An imperfect body had never seemed so irresistible to him. She walked past less than three feet from him without stopping. But when she was close to him, she suddenly turned her head, looked him in the eye and stuck out her tongue.

That mouth, he thought.

It was the most disproportionate thing about her. She had the lips of someone twice her size, buck teeth, everything moist and warm. It was the first time in years that something so far removed from asceticism had excited him. The flight of one of the jacks bisected their line of sight, separating them. He was about to walk on when a new question made him stop.

'Will you be leaving tomorrow?'

He nodded, not taking his eyes off the two fair-skinned bodies that had already turned the corner at the end of a poorly lit block, like grotesque mirrors of the possible results of the same womb.

'Wait another day. Mark my words, the rains are coming.'

'Rain, here?'

'Ask people in town if you don't believe me.'

He didn't do it. He spoke to no one that evening.

Fifteen minutes later, at a corner table in the general store, he was eating without taking his eyes off the plate of bland lentils. To his disappointment, the blondes were nowhere to be seen. The specimens squawking around him were as far removed from his race as he'd seen in months, and that despite the fact that the mixing of races in Buenos Aires was beginning to reach a level of no return. There was no end of genetic cleansing they could do. He'd said that to the General at one of the many parties to which he had been invited.

'If you want to do something for your country, ban the mixing of races.'

Everybody laughed, taking his proposals as a joke. But nothing daunted him and there were few who had the necessary courage to ban the mixing of races. *Blessed be the faith of those who dare to reform the face of the world in pursuit of their own ideal*, he thought, but he didn't dare cite La Rochelle in the presence of the General, who was already raising his glass to welcome the newcomers, instead he murmured, his teeth drowned in champagne: *With the pride of the mature races, our powerful obedience accepted the pain of bearing in our blood this invasion of the greatness of the world.*

He had for years scribbled his favourite quotations in the margin of his notebooks. That night the faces around him confirmed to him that there were many regions of the world in which they were losing the battle. They did not see the damage that mixing the races was doing to their continent. Sometimes it's too late to avoid the damage done to heritage, genes, genealogy. They talk about class in schools, never about race… two separate things.

He was in bed before eight o'clock.

The possibility of not seeing the blondes again kept him awake until he reached for one of his notebooks to draw the measurements of their bodies. He recalled them from memory, without a shred of doubt. He could imagine their bone structures, the volume of their organs, their jawbones and the composition of their blood flow. But he would never be able to lay the two out on metal trays to compare them. For a man used to getting what he wanted, the possibility of not seeing them again was intolerable. He had lived in this far corner of the world for almost a decade and he even caught himself thinking in Spanish. He had arrived from Geneva with the clothes on his back and a small bag containing his greatest treasures: three notebooks filled with writing about the last years of study on human experiments and a few blood samples in glass containers. A customs official had asked him what they were.

'Biological annotations,' he had answered in German.

'What kind?'

'Animal experiments.'

They detained him while they awaited the arrival of the port's veterinary doctor, to whom he described in great detail his experiments with cows that allowed him, on demand, to produce twin calves. He omitted that in the Kaiser-Wilhelm-Institut they wanted to produce the systematic birth of twins in women to increase twofold the growth of the race. Nor that in a moment of optimism he had sworn that pregnancy would be reduced to 135 days. His insistence convinced the veterinarian as to the advantages afforded by two identical animals as a privileged field of research which allowed for the reproduction of specific qualities or bodily defects. After years of comparing twin calves, using one of them as a control, he had discovered which attributes and weaknesses they inherited genetically and which ones came from their environment. Argentina was the ideal country to pursue his study, and perhaps he would come to discover the key to multiple births and thus accelerate the proliferation of the bovine race. Taken aback by the superabundance of information, the official, who barely spoke German, allowed him in without even confiscating his samples. The chaos at the port was too large to start worrying about a doctor entering the country with a Red Cross passport.

'Well, you'll have fun here,' an official who came from a German family and who had heard everything said, before stamping the document. 'I mean, in terms of cows.'

'Are there a lot?'

'Millions.'

'That many?'

'Can you really make them give birth two at a time?'

'Everything is possible.'

'Then we could feed the entire world.'

He smiled and made his way through the throng of recent arrivals. Once he was installed in a hotel room in Palermo, he ceased to talk about his life with the same discreet elegance used by so many of his colleagues who forgot to mention him during the trials… Why bother to mention him, after all, if they thought he was dead? He had undertaken to vanish into thin air without a trace, never giving in to the temptation to lower his guard, to the point of forfeiting for over a decade any contact with his son. The only time he saw him before going into exile on the other side of the ocean, he ordered the intimate circle organising the visit to tell the child it was his Uncle Fritz and not his father who was going to walk home from school with him. Once in Argentina, he never once wrote him or sent a telegram. He knew his survival depended on discipline. After a few months he was lodged in a rented room in a house in Olivos, divorced from any correspondence with the mother of his son, who had refused to leave with him. She was one of the many people in his intimate circle who, upon learning of his successes, called them atrocities.

Free of excess baggage, there was no reason to return.

He was not going to find any other country that would welcome a man like him with more open arms. Within two years he had found employment with a pharmaceutical company, bought a two-storey house in Vicente López, married his brother's widow, thus duplicating with this union a million-dollar inheritance. He had even gone so far as to list himself in the telephone book under his real name. He had no need to go under a surgeon's knife or change his name as so many others had.

But the illusion of a new life didn't last long. At every get-together he was reminded that the bloodhounds were getting closer and closer. He had asked himself hundreds of times how to go on after the defeat. The survivors were hiding out in every corner of the earth, pursued like criminals. He could feel around his neck the noose they had used to hang so many others, hunted down like wild animals, huddling together in the middle of the night, judged and condemned from across the ocean before being massacred. And the worst part was that no one raised a voice to defend them. They were alone.

He swore he was not going to end up like that.

2

The next morning, having flexed his arms 200 times to eliminate the last chemical fibres of the tranquilizer he had taken, he was filling his car at a petrol station a few yards from the desert motorway when he saw the girl from the day before get out of a Citroën filled with suitcases, unaware that her favourite doll (the realistic replica of a six-month-old baby) fell on its head on the pavement as she ran toward the small market. He drew close enough to cover the perfect body of the doll with his shadow. Its mouth was half-open and behind some lips, painted by the sure hand of an artisan, he could see a small red tongue. He bent down to pick it up. He put one hand behind the neck of the doll and the other on its left heel, as he had done with so many others that were breathing. He studied it front and back. It was a baby made of porcelain, with skin that had been polished to give it the softness of a newborn. His clinical eye could discern some imperfections, tiny traces that indicated it had been made by an artisan, although undoubtedly he had used an imported doll as a mould, one similar to the ones he'd seen in the arms of high-born little German girls. An almost imperceptible tick-tock caused him to raise the doll to his left ear... Was it a watch? It took him only a moment to confirm that, yes, it was. It beat inside the porcelain doll, attached to the inside of the chest. The effect was unsettling. The doll had a mechanical heart. He had never before studied one so closely. It was a work of art that was too close to real life.

'It's mine.'

He smiled before raising his head. The authority of the voice of children, for someone who knew how to listen, was always mixed with strands of horror. Moreover, this one had tiny traces of the deformed body to which it belonged. Even though it was deeper that he would have expected, it was too nasal, too sharp, too uneven. Standing in front of him with her arms akimbo, Lilith confronted him with all four feet of her height. He was still down on his heels, but he was kind enough to bend his back a few inches so he wouldn't be towering over her. He was used to weighing and measuring a body just by looking at it. She was probably eight years old, weighed sixty-five pounds, was well fed and had perfect teeth. Her clothes were old but clean and her skin, fingernails and hair showed no vitamin deficiencies.

'Where's she from?'

'My baby?'

'Where did you buy her?'

'We didn't buy her. My father made it.'

'Your father makes dolls?

'Sometimes.'

'What's her name?'

The stranger immediately made Lilith feel like she trusted him. She was not the first to be enchanted by his voice. She smiled at the way he looked fascinated at her doll.

'Herlitzka.'

'Her…?'

'…*litzka*.'

'Is it Russian?'

'She's female.'

'I mean the name.'

'No, she's Argentine. Just like me.'

'Aha,' he said with a German accent.

'Can I have her back?'

'Of course. She's yours.'

With considerable delicacy, as though handling a newborn, the German set the doll in the girl's arms.

'There's a clock inside her.'

'A heart.'

'When does it stop beating?'

'Not for a while.'

José nodded, keeping in check his desire to pursue the issue.

'Is she your daughter?'

Lilith hesitated a moment before nodding yes, as if deciding it then and there.

'Do you have any…?'

'Children?'

'Isn't that what we're talking about?'

She began to treat him like an idiot, even though she was delighted to explain her life to him. She had forgotten her mother's order not to separate from her brother.

'I shouldn't be talking to you.'

'Why not?'

'I'm not supposed to talk to strangers,' she said and smiled with the pearly sweetness of a nymph.

'Then we should say goodbye.'

The child nodded in agreement but didn't budge an inch. On the contrary, she slowly studied him, smiling like an accomplice.

'Momma says that it's enough for her to tell me not to do something for me to do it.'

'Is she right?'

'Mostly.'

'What part isn't true?'

'There're things I'd do anyway, even if I wasn't supposed to.'

'Would you be talking to me even if you weren't supposed to?'

'I think so.'

'But you're not sure…'

'Yes. I'm sure.'

She showed no fear of pauses and silences. She didn't even look away when the stranger smiled at her, looking her up and down. As if origins contained the key to everything, he repeated:

'How did you come up with that name?'

'It was my grandmother's favourite name. They wanted to call me Herlitzka, but my father said no.'

'And so they called you Lilly…'

'It's Lili*th*, with a *th*,' the small child said, delighted to contradict him. 'It means night monster.'

It means a lot more than that, the German thought.

God of darkness, libidinous goddess possessed by melancholy, transgression and desire… But there was no time to explain to her the power of her name. Their encounter could be interrupted at any moment and the fact that it was so ephemeral is what made it all the more enchanting. It had just struck him why her deformity was so upsetting: it was almost imperceptible, but marked her body inescapably. Her arms and legs were barely a few inches longer than normal. Her head was about an inch too big in circumference. Her eyes, mouth and ears suffered from the same delightful phenomenon, a mixture of nymph and goblin. The German held back the impulse to reach out and feel the shape of her head.

'Anyway, I'm too old to play with dolls.'

'Too old?'

'How old do you think I am?'

'Nine,' he lied, tacking an extra year on.

'I'm twelve.'

'Sorry about that.'

'That's OK. I'm used to it.'

'To what?'

'Being a lot older than people think.'

Holding his gaze, Lilith stretched her hand out toward his teeth, as if wanting to touch them. With a gesture of immodest indecency she crossed the threshold of his lips and rested the tip of her index finger on the tiny gap he had between his two front teeth.

'You have a gap between your teeth.'

'I know.'

'See? You're not perfect either.'

Many people said that obvious space between his top front teeth was the only imperfection he tolerated, his personal trademark. But no one had ever dared to mention it, much less to touch it. None of the women who had come close to his mouth had, either out of their own will or because they had been forced to, touched that gap with their tongues. Lilith smiled with a demented shine in her eyes (even the colour of her iris was unique, a mixture of grey and yellow) and he suddenly saw in them something old. It made him think she was more than twelve years old. She seemed aware of sticking her finger in the wolf's mouth. She rubbed the wet tip of her index finger against her thumb, covering it with the saliva of the stranger. Her act, far from annoying him, excited him in an unexpected way, with more intensity than the last sexual encounters he'd had, with a couple of employees at the pharmaceutical plant where he worked.

'Can you whistle through your teeth?'

'Whistle?'

He liked the sound of the word, but he didn't understand its meaning until Lilith puckered her lips and whistled. Despite the number of years he'd spent in Argentina, his vocabulary was still small and he had unexpected gaps. Like this one, one of his favourite hobbies, whistling, whose Spanish translation he had not yet learned.

'Ah… *pfeifen*,' he said and then whistled.

Obeying the call, a humid wind suddenly enveloped them, fluttering the skirt of Lilith's flowery dress with the first deformed notes. The man, by contrast, had nothing that could be moved by the wind. Everything about him was stuck to his body, slicked back and neat. Or that's what he thought, until he saw the directness with which Lilith rested a hand on her legs to keep the dress from dancing about and with the other brushed back a lock of hair that covered her eye, while she whistled through a narrow hole between two baby teeth. It wasn't the first time that a monstrous specimen had excited him in this way. Without thinking he responded to her whistling with a second melody that interwove with Lilith's, at first softly and then stronger and stronger and it drowned hers out.

There's music to be found even in the most unexpected places, he thought.

(And even his cynicism was by now a stammer.)

'Let's go, Lilith!'

Her brother's shout interrupted everything, past, present and future. José would have shot him on the spot if he'd had a gun.

'Lilith!'

He continued to whistle until the boy swooped down on his sister to grab her by the arm. But he had his hands full of shopping bags and no arms to force his orders. Totally captivated by him, Lilith joined in the last flourish of his tune, which ended on a sustained note. She bowed to him, resting the tip of her left foot on the tarmac, behind the right one, and at the same time she bowed her head and the doll's in his direction.

'Are you deaf or something?' her brother shook her. 'Get going.'

Deaf, no, he thought, *but she has no ears for you.*

As though she could hear the stranger who had hypnotized her, Lilith giggled in a way that sealed their complicity.

'That's Tomás, my prison guard,' she said pointing to her brother.

'Get going.'

'It was a pleasure to meet you Lili. My name's José.'

Only then did he stand up, but not without first stopping at the level of her left ear.

'And I can whistle a lot better than that,' he whispered. 'Some day I'll show you.'

Lilith hugged Herlitzka to her chest and shrugged her shoulders, biting her lip to keep from smiling. The tickle of the stranger's words caressed her ear and made its way in, descending through her throat down to between her legs. Her brother gave her a shove in the direction of the car.

'March.'

'Are you heading south?' he asked, in no hurry for them to leave.

'As far as Bariloche.'

'Could we go in convoy? They tell me the route through the desert is…'

'The route of death,' the boy interrupted him, smiling, as if it were a question of adventure and not a danger. 'Some 200 miles of nothing. Ask my father.'

He deposited a couple of bags in his sister's arms and pulled her by the hand toward the car. Only then did the German spot their father, whom he had taken for a petrol station employee. He was a *homo syriacus* with a round head, brachycephalic with a Jewish nose, a short body and stocky.

He was a bit overweight, normal stature, with a bald spot in the middle of his head. Sweat made his shirt stick to his body. The mother waited in the passenger seat, fanning herself. She was four months pregnant. She was as common as her husband, but she was clearly a *homo arabicus*, dolichocephalic, with a longish head. José's surprise came to a head when he discovered a young male about five years old as perfect as his older brother, playing with an English mastiff in the back seat. The two seemed to have eluded genealogical mandates: they were *homo europeans*, tall and thin, with whiter skin and clearer eyes than their parents. It wasn't the first time he had observed the same phenomenon: the genetics of two medio-cre individuals could combine to bring perfect specimens into the world. The combination irritated him because it defied his theories of cleansing. For more than a decade, in each one of the 3,000 twins who passed through his hands, he had attempted to demonstrate the complete and reliable classifi-cation of human genetics, along with the dimension of the damage wrought by unfavourable genetics.

'Dad, the gentleman wants to travel with us.'

'In my own car,' José hastened to add, pointing to a Chevrolet parked a few feet away. 'Following you, if it's no bother…'

The father took note of the neat appearance of the stranger and wiped the palm of his hands on his trousers. He'd been travelling this route for years and he'd never seen so much ele-gance in the middle of so much dust. He'd met foreigners, of course, poor guys intent on hiding their poverty and rich ones who pretended to be nobodies. They rarely travelled alone.

'Foreigners are always afraid of the route. But people still stop. If they see a car pulled over, they'll stop. Don't worry. And now that they're paving it, it will be better yet. You'll see the difference with the stretch that's still dirt.'

'Is there a lot that's still unpaved?'

'More than half.'

'That much?'

'Well, progress comes... but it comes slow. The important thing is not to be on it at night. If we leave now we'll arrive at dusk. Do you prefer to go in front or behind?'

'Behind, please.'

'Taking up the rear,' the fat man said, a model of friendliness.

José didn't drop his smile during the entire exchange. He feigned calm, but he would have begged if he'd had to. He could hardly recognise himself, because he hadn't discovered what a coward he was until after he stopped giving orders. They shook hands, each holding the other's gaze, without realising that it was all written there in the flesh that covered their bones: the scavenger-like firmness of a man on the run and the squishy confidence of a family man incapable even of killing the cockroaches that he often discovered in the corners of his house.

'We'd better get going.'

Eva's voice sounded strong and clear from inside the car. José leaned over a few inches to offer her his hand. That's when he saw the determination in the eyes of the woman, who was still quite young.

'My pleasure... Your children are beautiful.'

Eva smiled back wordlessly, as though she had no time for such pleasantries. She looked toward the sky, which was quickly clouding over.

'We'd better get going... Did you buy supplies?'

José looked at her startled. Eva had said the last sentence in perfect German, with no trace of a foreign accent. He thought for a moment he'd imagined it.

'I had breakfast an hour ago,' he said.

'Nevertheless, my advice is that you do.'

But it was true: they were speaking the same language. Eva's nervousness was not for the climate, but for the turns of destiny that had in an instant transported her back to her childhood home.

'How is it that you speak –'

'I went to a German school,' she cut him off.

'In Buenos Aires?'

'Bariloche.'

Like a bad joke, the harsh realities of life intruded on the memories of her childhood, because Primo Capraro had been much more than a school.

3

When he was advised to leave Buenos Aires immediately, they had promised him at the same time that the south of Argentina was as close as he could get to German Switzerland. They spoke to him of trees, lakes and snow-covered mountains. *You people were not the only ones who did a good job of cleansing*, they said. They told him stories of Indian attacks that had dominated the same arid lands he was now crossing at a snail's pace, with his eyes glued to the three small blonde heads examining him out of the corner of their eyes over the edge of the seats of the car in front. The only thing that stretched out before him was a straight line without the slightest bifurcation, with a desert of infertile land on either side. He felt anguish crawling up his legs like spiders. You could go crazy in a place like this, alone, without anything to do for hours, days and months on end. In such a barren place he could not imagine that he would ever see water again. Now he understood why so many people hesitated to cross Argentina except by train or boat; he had not believed them when they said that half of Argentina was a desert.

'You'll see there's nothing,' they said.

He had familiarized himself with the villages of Europe, in case his exile turned into a flight from one to the other. Here nothing meant *nothing*. Barely three shade-free farmhouses in more than a dozen miles. There wasn't a tree to be seen, barely a few dried-up bushes that the wind uprooted every time it blew hard. He had counted no more than one cow and one goat, all skin and bones, barely able to yield half a cup of milk. He saw a boy standing on the edge of the road, barefoot, watching them go by with a blank stare. A woman was hanging clothes out to dry, they looked dirty even from a distance. He moved his head in circles to stop himself getting a cramp. His eyelids began to feel weighed down. He found himself talking aloud more than once, dazed by the buzz of the wind hitting the windows with so much force that the gusts brought with them bits of bushes. An hour out, the first drops began to fall. The sky grew dark in a matter of minutes, with clouds that grew blacker and blacker, bursting with thunder and lightning.

By two o'clock it was night.

The Citroën slowed down to a walking pace, but it didn't come to a halt until the drops that burst against the windshield like bullets had turned into hail. One of the chunks struck the upper left edge of the windshield, causing a crack that, in just a few seconds, cut across the length of the glass. José gripped the steering wheel with both hands to keep the car from spinning like a top over the side of the road, which by that time was nothing but mud. *The worst catastrophes always begin like this*, he thought. *You don't even see them coming.*

He stopped a few feet from the Citroën.

With his index finger he brushed back a stiff lock of hair. He tried to see what was going on inside the other car. Enzo was gripping the steering wheel just like he was. Eva was waving her arms and shouting. She intrigued him, with her German, her pregnancy, her perfect sons… More than anything else, the charming abnormality of her only daughter. Thinking what the fourth child would be like produced in him an irresistible curiosity, whether it would tip the scale toward perfection or abnormality. In previous years he would have immediately ordered her to be placed on a stretcher so he could open her womb on the spot. It irritated him more than the hail, which

28

by then had begun to shake the whole car, not to be able to do what he wanted with the bodies of those around him. When the Citroën began to move again, he carefully followed every one of its movements, turning on his high beams and doing a U-turn to go back the way they'd come. Without rolling his window down even a fraction of an inch, Enzo motioned for him to follow. Eva was holding her youngest child in her arms and was staring straight ahead. The English mastiff was at the other window, barking like mad and banging his head against the glass, fighting the onslaught of the hail. There was little doubt in his mind as to what would happen if one of those projectiles of ice were to hit someone in the head. He could make Lilith out in the back seat, hugging Herlitzka and whispering in the doll's ear. She wasn't smiling anymore. Adventure had given way to fear.

It took them half an hour to go less than a mile, until the carcass of a burnt-out car, resting on four stakes a metre off the ground, indicated to them the exact spot to leave the road and drive into the open desert. The two cars moved ahead, almost on top of each other now, with the front end of the Chevrolet almost touching the rear end of the Citroën. The curtain of water surrounding them devoured everything and they didn't see the farmhouse until they had almost ploughed into it. They would have flattened it if it hadn't been for the barking of five starving dogs that surrounded the car jumping up at the doors and causing them to slow down even more. You could see their ribs and there were bloody wounds from the hail.

'What are we going to do here?'

No one answered Lilith's murmur.

'I don't like this place.'

There was a barely visible shed made from sheets of metal that rocked in the storm. It was filled with old tools, pieces of iron and a rusting truck without tyres. With each blast of wind, a pair of clothes lines with washing hanging from them smacked the walls like whips. The result was a deafening concert of sounds, bangings, barking and bursts of thunder, each one more violent than the last. There was barely room for the two cars. José had no choice but to park the front half of the car under the shed. No one dared to get out, sitting there quiet for several minutes with the lights on and the motor running. From where he sat, José could see Lilith covering her ears to keep out the furious struggle between the English mastiff and two of the other dogs, separated by a closed window that served only to increase their fury, dirtying the window with blood each time they banged against it.

A shot stopped them.

They all leapt in their seats, although no one had been hit. The mastiff hid under the seat and the five dogs ran off in opposite directions. José opened the small case next to him on the floor inside the Chevrolet and removed a leather case from among the books and papers. With the steadiness of a soldier he determined the Colt was loaded before looking up.

Only then did he see a man and two children emerging from the heart of the storm, their heads and bodies covered with sheets of metal, an improvised armour that transformed them into a cross between medieval knights and beggars. The two children were carrying aluminum buckets filled with water and the man had a rifle. He was the only one to come as far as the shed. His dogs, which seemed as savage as hyenas, surrounded him without making a sound, wagging their tails and not daring to bark. A skinny sheepdog with a trickle of blood down its forehead moved in front of him as though to protect him. The man went around to the Citroën and leaned the rifle against one of the walls when he saw Lilith and her brothers looking at him wide-eyed. He motioned to his sons to go on towards the house, which shuddered with each new onslaught of the storm. The two did as they were told, and as he walked toward the car the man removed the rounded piece of metal he carried over his head. His skin was tanned and wrinkled, although he had the eyes of a young man. Enzo wiped the palms of his hands on his trousers, opened the door and got out of the Citroën.

'The storm caught you,' the man said by way of welcome.

His voice was dry and laconic.

'I apologise for our driving in without asking. As soon as it's over we'll be on our way, but we needed somewhere to get out of the storm…'

'And we needed water.'

'I see.'

'No you don't. No one who lives near water understands the desert. We've been dry as a bone for the last two months.'

The man looked toward the interior of José's car, where José was staring right at him, not even when trying to be humble could he lower his gaze in front of a peasant.

'He's with us,' Enzo said, holding his hand out.

'There are some so dirty that not even the water can get them clean…'

It wasn't a joke, although Enzo laughed too much, extending toward him his arm and the open palm of his hand, avoiding the whiplash of one of the clothes lines the man trapped with one of his hands and tied to a pole without taking his eyes off him.

'I don't have much to offer, but come on in if you want to.'

'That's not necessary. We'll wait here.'

'Well, this won't let up until tomorrow,' he pointed to the sky and continued. 'We're busy collecting water. It's a blessing. You've got little kids there.'

'My children.'

'Come on in then,' he insisted. 'At least there's a fire going.'

From the inside of the car, Lilith could see them moving their lips, but she couldn't hear a word. She gave the English mastiff a kick to shut him up. She saw the man motioning toward the house and looked in that direction. She saw a girl about fifteen years old leaning against the edge of the door under a plastic overhang, her hair down to her waist, with her skin as dark as the two men. Lilith's gaze rested on the seven-months pregnant belly sticking out from between a torn T-shirt and a pair of men's trousers.

Enzo opened the car door.

'Get out. We're going to wait inside. Move fast. It's let up a little.'

He was talking for the sake of talking. The downpour continued, although the hail only hurt now, instead of drawing blood. He helped his wife out of the car and covered her with one of the sheets of metal.

'Run! Come on!' he ordered his children.

The three ran off as fast as they could, screaming and shouting, weaving here and there to avoid the hail. The dogs followed them as if they were prey for the first few yards and one managed to bite off one of Herlitzka's feet and ran off as Lilith stopped for an instant in the rain to see the dog fleeing with the foot in his mouth. Upset, she looked down at the doll, lame before taking her first step. But a direct hit on the back of her neck from a piece of hail made her start running again towards the house. Inside the car, José smiled with fascination at each one of her actions. Even when she was upset, Lilith was a delight. A banging on the window startled him out of his enchantment. Enzo was calling to him from outside the car. He stuck the Colt in his trousers before grabbing his case and broad-brimmed imported hat which, with only slight inclination of his chin, was wide enough to hide his eyes. Outside everyone was shouting to make themselves heard above the storm.

'What are we going to do?'

'Wait!' Enzo shouted. 'Until it lets up.'

'What if we're still here when night comes?'

Enzo shrugged his shoulders, overwhelmed by the situation, red-faced at his impotence. But José was as rigid as a stake, his hat on his head and his hands in his pockets. He was coldly evaluating his options, without blinking. From where he stood the owner of the house could barely see or make out his accent, so loud was the pounding of the stones of ice against the roof of the shed. Enzo turned toward him.

'I would introduce you,' he shouted. 'But I don't know his name.'

'That's all to the good,' the owner said. 'The less you know about people, the better.'

He, by contrast, did not raise his voice for a second. It was impossible to hear him, and Enzo had to read his lips.

Inside the house, standing in front of a dying fire, the teenager tore yellowing pages from a book one page at a time, which she balled up before throwing on the fire. She was standing barefoot on the dirt floor, with a damp rag hanging from her pocket. A half-dozen balls of paper were enough to bring the fire back to life. She set the book on a pile of others awaiting their turn to be ripped apart and used the damp rag to wipe the book's leather cover. Standing about a yard away and avoiding looking her in the eye, Lilith managed to read the title, *Science of the Mapuches*. She turned to look at a small altar containing a hand-painted plaster statue, surrounded by three candles, burned down to an inch in height. The offerings were desert rocks, stones like the ones piled up as far as the eye could see, the teenage girl cleaned them with special care, one by one, as if they were relics. Lilith looked up at the ceiling where two legs of ham and a dozen sausages hung. The adults continued to talk behind her back in sentences that lapsed into silence, over and over again. They were lousy conversationalists, all except for José, the only one who kept his mouth shut. He looked at them wondering how it was possible that a people of a bastard race, with mixtures so opposite and undesirable, had managed to survive for thousands of years in such inhospitable conditions in the face of constant persecution. It was a genetically degenerate race because of the poison of the mixture, inculcated over more than 2,000 years in their blood, drop by drop…

No wonder Darwin called this a cursed land, he thought.

Almost all the Latin races had been born of this mixing, children of hybridity. There they were, oblivious to the racial sin that mixture was, although the animal-like features of the inferior races made it clear. Enzo's nose, Eva's obesity, Lilith's dwarfism, the skin colour of the owners of the house. The sin committed against the laws of sacred harmonies was there, engraved on their faces and bodies… Indelibly. A *cloaca gentium*, a point of encounter for the bastards of the world.

'How come you decided to set out today?' the owner of the house asked, courtesy and social formulas having been exhausted.

'We had no idea,' Eva said.

'They don't have to broadcast it for you to see a storm is coming,' the owner answered as he took a kettle out of the fire. 'Take a seat.'

The gesture was enough for the two men to remove the clothes and dishes stacked up on the four chairs. Eva obeyed because that's what she had heard: an order. And it was not difficult, she thought, to guess that everyone there obeyed in silence.

She was wrong.

The silence was the result of the presence of so many strangers in a house that hadn't seen visitors for years. It was neither fear nor submission. If that man had achieved anything, it was to invent for them a whole world within four walls and supports of the abode. But no one who lived there knew how to deal with visitors, what to offer them and what to say to them. The teenager buried the tip of a dry twig in the fire and used it to light three of the candles, while the two men poured the containers of rainwater into a metal basin. Everyone was uncomfortable and had no idea of what to do or say, all except for Lilith, who approached the altar. She stood next to the teenager and observed her in silence, following the rhythm of the twig as it went from one candle to the other.

'Who is it?'

The teenager looked at the owner of the house out of the corner of her eye. The man nodded as he continued to prepare the *maté*.

'Ngenechen,' the girl said, so low that only Lilith heard her.

'A saint?'

'A god,' the man said.

'Whose god?'

'That's enough, Lilith,' Eva cut her off.

But she didn't look at her mother, but rather at the owner of the house.

'Mapuche.'

'Ah, those are the Indians they killed…?'

'Not all of them,' the man said and smiled.

The teenager went outside and returned a few seconds later with an armload of pieces of damp wood piled up under the

35

overhang, covered in toadstools. She used the curve of her belly to keep the load from slipping to the floor. She selected the five largest pieces and placed them one by one on the fire. Lilith followed the path of each spark that flashed between her bare feet, and the teenager appeared to feel nothing.

'Her name is Yanka,' the man said when he saw how Lilith was staring at her and pointed to the two boys. 'Lemún and Nahuel.'

'And what's your name?'

'And what's your name, *sir*,' Eva corrected.

'And what's your name, sir?' Lilith asked smiling.

'Cumín.'

'What does that mean?'

'How do you know it means anything?'

'Strange names always mean something.'

'Red tiger.'

'See.'

Cumín smiled back at her. She was the only one he liked. There was no trace of malice in her questions. Behind his back, Enzo could not keep still. He paced back and forth trying to calm his younger son, who was crying. He hadn't stopped crying since they'd got out of the car. Everything frightened him: the storm, the hail, the dogs, the hungry stares of these strangers... They also made Tomás hold back. He remained standing by the doorway, ready to run off.

'It's getting dark, dad,' he said in one of the many moments of silence, and the obviousness of the comment made the two brothers smile. For some time they had been looking at him like two wild cats eye a city mouse.

Although it was still early, the storm had made the sky dark for hours.

'I know.'

'You said we shouldn't be on the road at night.'

'I know what I said, Tomás!'

His yelling made the baby cry harder than ever. Exasperated, he put the child in Eva's arms.

'Five years travelling this road from one end to the other and never once did it rain…'

'Calm down, Enzo.'

'Have you ever seen hail, Cumín?'

'Around here? Never.'

A clap of thunder crowned the sentence, followed by the baying of one of the dogs, half mad by now. He sucked up the last drop of *maté* before making a new one.

'But things are changing,' he said.

The baying of the dog was joined by two others, a disjointed chorus that seemed directed at the moon.

'See? Even my dogs are wolves…'

Cumín couldn't resist it and smiled. He found the situation entertaining.

'No need for you to worry. You can spend the night here and continue on your way tomorrow. In reality, you have no choice. So say yes and let's talk about something else.'

'I appreciate it.'

'Don't thank me, but tell me what's going on out in the world. Not even the radio works here. And time…' He pointed to a clock on the wall barely visible beneath some coats. 'We brought it with us when we moved here. But it stopped working and so we don't even have that.'

Lilith saw that it was stopped at three in the morning.

'And how do you know what time it is?' she asked.

'We don't. Not even if today is Friday or Saturday.'

'It's Sunday.'

'I told you,' Lemún said under his breath. 'Now it's your turn.'

He shoved Nahuel, who went outside without a word and disappeared into the storm. Lilith looked at her younger brother, who was crying harder than ever, choking on his own tears.

'Don't be afraid,' she whispered in his ear. 'Nothing's going to happen.'

Lemún and Yanka exchanged glances and then looked at Cumín, who smiled as he cut down three of the sausages hanging from the room and set them over the fire.

'I always tell them the opposite.'

'That they should be afraid?'

He nodded, arranging the sausages on the fire.

'You shouldn't tell them not to be afraid... Maybe you think monsters don't exist?'

'Do they?'

'Of course... Maybe they're not under the bed, but there's no question they're right around the corner.'

'There're no corners here,' Lilith said without missing a beat.

Cumín saw that the man in the hat was smiling as he looked at her. He was the only one who made him mistrustful. Even his smile was icy. He looked like a robot wearing a mask, furtive, unhuman, rigid like a stick of wood covered in clothing. Empty.

Empty of what? Cumín asked himself.

Himself, he replied. *There's no one there.*

But that couldn't be. No one is completely empty unless he's a corpse. And you couldn't see death in that man's eyes just yet. What he could see was a look he had already seen when he was a child, when he still had nothing, not even a patch of dirt. He could read the scorn underneath the display of false cordiality.

José felt the wind and cold seeping in through the pieces of nylon that covered the windows and he moved a couple of feet away when he felt the water splattering his feet. He couldn't stand having been brought up in the cultural and artistic centre of the world, only to end up hiding out in a hole like this. It was entirely his fault. He was the one to insist on following the dirt road when they had offered him a train compartment and someone to meet him at the station at the end of his trip. The fear they would find him was too great. The key to survival was not to trust a soul and to fade into thin air without leaving a trace.

'Why don't you sit down,' Cumín said. It wasn't a question.

José obeyed. He was beginning to pay greater attention to the owner of the house. He could let them burn his books to make a fire, but he thought like a man who read or who had read. There were flickerings in the faces of his sons who, in some way, had managed to escape the flatness around them. They could imagine things, and each one had his own imagination. They hadn't been there very long. They were also fleeing from something. That was the sort of thing José could make out by looking someone in the eyes. Before answering, Cumín took the sausages out of the fire and cut them in pieces that he placed on a wooden plank.

'So, you're travelling together?'

'No, not really,' Enzo replied, noting how the German stood silently off to the side with no intention whatever of talking to anyone. 'We just met a couple hours ago.'

'So, you've been brought together by fear…'

'This gentleman's fear,' Eva said, referring to José.

'Amen,' Lilith whispered.

Cumín laughed out loud and patted her on the head with a greasy hand, totally smitten. He went over to José to offer him a piece of meat, but he wouldn't take no for an answer when the man shook his head.

'Taste it.'

'I don't eat meat,' José said, without looking him in the face.

It was the first time he'd opened his mouth. His voice sounded hoarse after so many hours of not talking. Cumín turned toward him and stood looking at him in silence for a few moments, a pause that froze all of them in a void and froze José's blood. He looked at him with no sign of surprise, as if confirming what he already suspected. José had already come across people in the interior of the country who barely knew what was going on in the rest of the world.

The war? they asked… *Since when?*

But this man was different. Even living at the end of the world.

'They're pork,' he said, thrusting the plank a little more in his direction.

José had no choice so chose the smallest piece and put it in his mouth with evident mistrust. Cumín waited until he had chewed it three, four, five times and swallowed before moving, looking at him with a smile that made it seem like he found his fear entertaining.

'Do you like it?'

He nodded he did, sickened by the taste.

'You must have tasted some like it in your country.'

'I can't recall.'

'Oh but you must have. Would you like more?'

'No, thanks.'

'One thing you can find a lot of over there are pigs.'

He speared two pieces for Yanka, who was watching him without moving.

'Eat.'

'I'm not hungry.'

'He is,' he said, pointing at her belly with the knife.

He watched her chew and did not move until he saw her swallow. He turned away and set the plank on the table in front of Eva and Enzo.

'This was our last animal, the first Lemún was to butcher on his own. We were keeping it for a special occasion…'

'No, thanks.'

'Go ahead,' he insisted.

He spoke still holding the knife in his hand, gesturing with it as he spoke. José could not believe the display of germs he was witnessing. The *maté* went from mouth to mouth, the metal straw covered with microscopic remains of saliva, tea and sausage. One of the pieces was large enough for Yanka to remove it with a fingernail before taking the straw in her own mouth. Thunderstruck, he watched her chew a piece of sausage as she drew on the straw. He resisted the temptation to take out one of his notebooks on the spot and jot down the exquisite variety of bodies that paraded before his eyes. A circus sideshow: skins, bones and organs of all sizes and colours, deformities, pregnancies, blood ties… Two opposing but complete genealogical trees: success with blondes, failure with the dwarf, mediocrity with the adults, animalism in the dark skinned ones and even incest… Where else could that second bulging belly have come from here in the middle of the desert except from the father or one of the sons?

'How far along are you?' he asked Eva in German.

'Seventeen weeks.'

She answered in Spanish, as if wanting to make clear that she wasn't his accomplice, that they shared nothing beyond the road through the desert. She'd been uncomfortable for some time with the look of the stranger, who studied her openly. She saw him shift his interest toward the other pregnant woman, who was serving *maté* to them in aluminium cups. He realised he was going too far with his question, but he was quite taken in.

'And you?' he challenged.

Yanka looked up at him.

'How far along are you?'

'Who said she was pregnant?'

Cumín's question brought him up short.

Everyone fell silent again.

Nahuel walked in at that moment, with a splotch of hail on his forehead. He set Herlitzka's chewed-up foot on the table. It was almost impossible to make out the toes and was more a clump of mud with a dozen teeth marks. He walked over to the fire to shed his soaking-wet clothes with Yanka's help, who wrung out each item in a corner before placing it over a clothes line two yards from the fire, smoking it at the same time it dried it. Nahuel's only gesture of modesty when he saw he was being observed by foreign eyes was to take a step backward so that half his body was hidden by a tattered piece of cloth that served as a divider. But it was enough just to step forward a bit, as José did, just a twist of the body, to violate any desire for intimacy. He observed him with furrowed brow, just as he did each time a new object of study was put in front of him. The boy was as trim as could be, not a bit of fat, all fiber, pronounced muscles and hunger… years of hunger. Enzo's chubby arm crossed his line of vision. He grabbed a piece of sausage and popped it in his mouth, savouring the taste.

'Um, this tastes good, by God…'

'And to think that pig had nothing but air to eat.'

'What do you mean "air"?' Lilith asked.

'It's a manner of speaking, silly,' Tomás said.

'I don't understand, what does it mean?'

'That everyone's starving to death here.'

'Tomás!'

His mother's shushing made him shut up. There was no evil in his comment, although Lemún's skin burned with anger or humiliation. Enzo sighed. It didn't make any sense trying to keep a conversation going here. And they still had the whole night ahead. For a moment the only thing you could hear was the hail hitting the tin roof and the dozen sounds of leaking drops of water falling into containers scattered around the place. Tomás felt a knot in his throat and the desire to laugh and cry at the same time, a mixture of shame and power coming from the first thrust of cruelty in anyone's life.

'Forgive him,' Enzo said, mortified. 'Sometimes he says dumb things.'

'What he says is true,' Cumín answered and turned to look at José. 'You asked me if there was any work.'

He went over to the door and opened it. Beyond the curtain of rain, the road they had come by was barely discernible.

'Doing road work,' Cumín went on, after bending over to pick up a piece of hail, which he put in his mouth as though it were candy. 'The road that will populate Patagonia…'

…*with people like you*, he added mentally.

For some strange reason everyone heard his thought clearly. It was something that happened often to Cumín and his family. At first it had been a surprise, then everyone's favourite game. They had in the last few months accepted it as something totally natural, like you accept a belief and yield to faith. They had a theory: the silence was so extreme in that corner of the world that on windless days you could hear everything, even what was not said.

'And you have no day off?' Enzo asked.

'Day off?'

'A day you don't work.'

'Whenever the truck doesn't show up for us… But it's not regular. Sometimes it shows up fifteen days in a row and then it won't come for a week. It depends on the material that comes from the quarries.

43

'And when the road is done, what will you do?' Lilith asked, with her usual facility for touching sore spots.

'There will always be roads to pave.'

'But will you move from one place to the other?' she insisted.

'If there's no other choice.'

Cumín answered her honestly, looking her in the eye like an adult. There was no cynicism in Lillith's words.

'That was the offer: land and work. They didn't tell me there was no shade and that it was slave labour. But something is better than nothing. The world functioned with slave labour since the time of the Romans, hasn't it?'

The last question was for the stranger who didn't even dare look him in the eye. José kept his eyes glued to the dirt floor. If they had met sometime in the past, he would have made sure those eyes never looked at anything again. This was the type of individual he preferred to dispose of from the start.

4

'Done,' Yanka said.

She pushed the last bit of glue into Herlitzka's foot. She had spent the last hour preparing the glue with pages from *Mapuche Science*, which she used to fill each one of the toes of the doll's foot, using a small wood stick. She destroyed the wisdom of her ancestors with no compunction. Her forefathers had taught her that everything must transform in order not to be lost. Lilith watched her in silence, both were seated near the open door, the only place where the air was less stuffy.

'I think it's useless… See?'

Yanka squeezed the piece of plastic to show her what was going on. Full of holes and teeth marks, Herlitzka's deformed foot was leaking white strands of glue all over the place. Night had already fallen outside, but the storm continued with the same force, soaking their clothes and faces a yard away from the door. Lilith could hear her father snoring. He was sleeping in the same cot with her mother and her younger brother. It was the sleep of a man under stress, and every two or three minutes apnea would jolt him awake and yank his wife and her child into consciousness, for just an instant, before sinking back into sleep. Cumín was also dozing, seated next to the fire. José was the only adult still awake. He was writing in a leather-bound notebook, although he was watching them the whole time out of the corner of his eye with growing interest in what they were doing. When he saw Lilith attempting to fill her doll's foot again, to no avail, he approached them with his suitcase in his hand.

'May I?' as he pointed to a nearby chair.

Lilith nodded without looking at him. When he saw her not getting anywhere, her legs, like those of Yanka, covered in glue, José sat down next to them, rolled his sleeves up and opened his suitcase.

'You have to sew it,' he said.

'How?'

'You have to close the holes and sew the foot to the body.'

'And who's going to do that?'

'I will.'

Lilith stood up with the foot in one hand and the doll in the other and approached José. She saw a dozen bottles and pill boxes inside the suitcase, in addition to a black case that José opened on the table, displaying all sorts of objects: a scalpel, a surgical blade, scissors, tweezers, needles, alcohol, bandages...

'How come you have all that?'

José selected the thickest needle and a very fine suture of the kind he used for deep wounds, which he held in front of his eyes with the tip of his thumb and index finger while he prepared the thread with his other hand.

'Are you a doctor?'

'A vet,' José said. 'And an anthropologist.'

He wasn't lying, thinking of his beginnings. He had defended his doctoral dissertation in 1935 with the title 'Morphological Study of Races Based on the Submaxillary Frontal Lobe', graduating with honours from the Department of Anthropology of the University of Munich. Barely three years later, in a medical thesis titled 'Studies on the Palatal Mandibular Labial Fissure in Certain Tribes', José was already demonstrating the importance of investigating twins. He threaded the needle at first attempt and opened a bottle of alcohol with which he moistened some gauze.

'Give it to me,' he ordered.

Lilith set the doll on the table and gave him the foot, which José cleaned inside and out before turning Herlitzka over, gripping her head between his legs. He moved the leg that was all right out of the way and left the damaged one pointing up in the air like a mast. Without concealing his pleasure, he moved the foot into the exact position he wanted, matching almost perfectly the two pieces of porcelain.

'You're going to have to hold her.'

Lilith moved over so she was only a few inches from him, close enough that José's knee brushed more than once against her pubis as he rotated the doll to find the best place to begin the suture. Lilith, taking seriously her role as nurse, held Herlitzka without trembling. She felt his breath on her face, bitter and sour like the smell of the tobacco her father smoked when he thought no one was looking.

'Squeeze a little bit here,' José said, wrapping the bandage around one more time.

'Like this?'

'Once more…'

José cut the bandage and carefully twitched the foot, which held firm.

'Now the stitches,' he said, as if talking about dessert.

He held the needle with the tip of his index finger and his thumb with the precision of a surgeon. He looked for a hole in the porcelain and inserted the bandage, pulling it through a hole in the leg and the places where the dogs had bitten to join the two pieces.

'You're from Bariloche?'

'My grandmother… She was, but she died. That's why we're going there.'

'For the funeral?'

'They buried her two months ago.'

'Then why bother to make the trip?'

'We're going to live in her house. It's a guesthouse.'

'*Mist*,' José said under his breath, the needle stuck in the tip of his thumb. He pulled it out and sucked a drop of blood. 'What were you saying?'

'She left it to us… The house.'

'Do you like it?'

'I spent every summer of my life there.'

José adjusted with his index finger the black-rimmed glasses he'd taken from the suitcase minutes before. He cut the filament of the first (perfect) stitch and went on to the next one, hiding the filament stitch behind the heel in a display of talent that made him feel more alive than anything had during the past few months of exile. He knew immediately that he had found a solution for his nostalgia. It was of no importance that the baby was porcelain. He could do what he wanted with it without raising anyone's suspicions. Lilith held her breath, her attention fixed on the dance of the needle as it wove in and out of the bandage, seeking out the holes made by the teeth and joining the foot to the rest of the body.

'It's a temporary fix… There are always scars.'

'We can always fire her again,' Lilith said, as if she made porcelain bodies every day.

José looked up in surprise.

'Who's going to do it?'

'My dad… He's the one who made Herlitzka.'

'He made the dolls?'

Lilith nodded.

'He says it's a hobby.'

That's when he knew what he had to do, as he made the final stitch. The seed of what was to come was planted right there, as he prepared a German spatula by dipping it into a plastic cup of Pampas-style glue. He filled the foot and shaped it to look like the undamaged one. If he'd had more instruments he would've changed the colour of the nails, from old rose to pearly salmon. He had once visited a doll factory decades before. He was enthralled by the plaster moulds and the possibility of making an infinite number of perfect bodies from the same mould. He told everyone at that stage he wanted to be a soldier, not a doctor, but he never forgot the image. Suddenly he was savouring the endless experiments that he would be able to do on porcelain babies.

'Done,' he said, holding his work up in front of Lilith's face.

An explosion of laughter from the three boys made Lilith jump. Tomás had won the friendship of Cumín's two sons the minute he took some comic books out of his trouser pocket. Seated by the fire, the two brothers had spent the last couple of hours looking at the pictures, fascinated by the world of caricature unfamiliar to them.

'What's that mean?' Nahuel asked, when the need to know what was being said by a squad of five soldiers who were firing on an uprising of Ranquele Indians overcame his need not to admit he couldn't read it.

'Where?'

'Here.'

Tomás hid his surprise, because for two hours they'd been pretending to read. Without asking anything else, he read. The laughter of the two brothers was cut short when they found in the midst of comic strips about Gringo cowboys, Romans and Greeks, a comic about soldiers and Indians set in the very desert in which they lived.

'It says that the Indian is like the heron, because it makes a song and dance to protect one place but its nest is somewhere

49

else…' Tomás pointed to a small balloon that floated above the head of one of the soldiers pointing his rifle at a row of women and old people. 'This guy is asking, *And if we know the chieftains are all assembled in one place what do we do?*' Then he pointed to the next balloon, in which another soldier answered before opening fire, '*We'll go to the Indians' village and take the rabble hostage!* is what it says. Then they open fire.'

'What does "rabble" mean?'

'I don't know.'

'The women,' Nahuel says.

'The women, the children and the old people,' Yanka said.

She'd joined them without their realising it and examined the comic strip over their shoulders. She pointed to the next frame.

'There they're killing everyone.'

'Why?' Nahuel asked.

'Your father already told you why.'

Tomás tried to close the comic, but Lemún had already grabbed it from his hands. The killing of the Indians continued in the next pages, along with the victories of a regiment of white men in blue uniforms covered in dust who dug a dirt ditch in the middle of the desert and sacked villages, burning them and then receiving medals as they embraced their children as war heroes…

'Where'd you get that?' Lemún asked.

'I bought it in Buenos Aires.'

'And who taught you that they killed the Indians?'

'I didn't say that.'

'Your sister said it.'

'Ask her.'

'If your sister knows it, you do, too.'

Tomás shrugged his shoulders, cornered.

'In school… Don't you go?'

'Where?'

'To school.'

'There's no school around here,' Nahuel said.

'And so you don't go because there's no school?'

'Where'd you like us to go?'

'Beats me… You're quick.'

They didn't answer him. Tomás stood up. He was getting more uncomfortable by the minute. He put his comic books away and put his hand out for the one Cumín's oldest son still had.

'OK…' his voice breaking on the final syllable, but he stumbled ahead so he wouldn't lose his nerve. 'I think I'm going to lie down for a while… Can I have the comic back?'

'I'm keeping this one.'

Lemún didn't look up from the comic book. He was trying to stop himself from hitting him. It's not that he didn't like the blonde kid, but the thought that they had been laughing at a couple of Gringo cowboys in just the previous comic… His father had always told him that one day he'd be angry for what they'd done to them. The last time, Nahuel had gone so far as to say, 'They didn't do anything to me.'

It was barely a whisper, his face staring down at the plate of stew set before him. But Cumín heard it as an insult.

'You don't think so?'

'No.'

'And who do you think you are? Without your great grandfather who do you think you'd be?'

'No one.'

He never had understood why his father got so angry about something that had happened more than a hundred years before. But there he was again, seated at the head of the table, his arm in the air and his eyes red with rage, as if his own children were the people who had made them leave Carmen de Patagones in the middle of the night. *You screamed at the wrong people*, an aunt who refused to remain with them told him, *you'd better watch your tongue*.

'Don't you think the extermination of all of the Indian peoples was a plan? Do you know what they said? That first they were going to exterminate the nomads and then those who lived in villages... But here we are. We have roots and we have land and no one exterminated us. We're the living proof of the failure of a project.'

He calmed his screaming with a gulp of spirits.

'Son of a bitch,' he continued under his breath.

And it was the perfect insult, almost something desirable, because a whore who had no interest in being a mother had given birth to him. He missed her every time he got drunk. He'd become filled with despair and say that he was sick and tired of the hole they lived in.

'It's not a hole. It's our house.'

'This isn't a house.'

'If you don't like it, why don't we leave?'

'Because we have nowhere to go.'

He had convinced himself they were already men.

He would say again and again, *if it were down to submissive types like you, they'd have killed us all*.

That night, looking at the caricature of an Indian wearing a loincloth and feathers, crying like a startled bird in front of a burning village, Lemún felt Cumín's rage.

'OK, I'll lend it to you,' Tomás said and his voice broke again. 'You'll give it back to me tomorrow?'

'No. I'm going to keep this one.'

'That's OK. I'll give it to you.'

He backed away and was about to sit down on one of the empty cots when Nahuel gestured at him.

'That's the one we sleep on.'

'Oh, so where should I…'

'Over there.'

He pointed to the cot where the rest of his family was sleeping on top of each other. Tomás nodded resignedly and sat down on the edge of the cot, leaned his back against the wall and closed his eyes. He couldn't wait for morning to come. Nahuel stood looking at him. He took his straight blade out of a pocket and continued to work on a piece of wood he was fashioning into a serpent. Every so often he looked up at Tomás… measuring the distance for a slash of the blade. He bit his lip and looked at his brother, who remained engrossed in the comic.

'Burn it.'

'Not on your life.'

'If Cumín were to see it…'

'He won't see it.'

'They won't get out of here if he does.'

'He won't see it,' he repeated. 'Don't say a thing.'

By the time things had become tense between the brothers, José had already sewn up half of Herlitzka's foot. The two pieces fit together perfectly. He allowed less than a millimetre between each stitch and he worked with such perfection that the suture became a very delicate ankle bracelet right above the heel. Lilith began to smile halfway through his work and when José put in the final stitch, she was ecstatic. She hugged Herlitzka, although the doll's feet were still sticking up in the air, as if the only thing that mattered from now on was the foot that had been amputated and reconstituted as if by magic. She watched José put his instruments away one by one without hiding her fascination.

'Will you teach me?'

'What?'

'To do what you just did.'

'To sew?'

'Yes.'

'It's late right now…'

'In Bariloche.'

'I don't know if we'll continue to see each other in Bariloche.'

'Yes,' Lilith said. 'I'm going to continue to see you.'

José smiled without looking at her as he closed the suitcase.

'Well, maybe then.'

'Promise?'

'When the disciple is ready, the master appears.'

'I'm prepared.'

This time he did look at her, surprised by the vehemence with which she spat each word out. He was convinced that their meeting had been a strange coincidence, almost magical, a synchronism, one of those accidents full of meaning, as Nietzsche would say. But not for the reasons Lilith thought.

'I can yank her other foot off.'

'What?'

'Herlitzka's other foot. I can cut it off, or one of her hands…'

'Why?' José asked astonished.

'To sew it back on again.'

His soulmate looked up smiling, only a few inches away, looking so grotesque and charming that he couldn't keep from removing a speck of glue a fraction of an inch from the edge of her mouth.

'We'll see. Now go on, get some sleep.'

He pointed to the only cot. They were too much by themselves and too close together to resist, but it wasn't the time or the place. And he was a patient man.

'And what about you?'

'I can rest sitting up. Go on.'

Lilith shrugged her shoulders and lay down next to Yanka. She continued to look at him, convinced that this man who had come from nowhere was going to vanish into thin air if she closed her eyes. When he saw that it was beginning to get light outside, José blew out the last candle and put his hat on before leaning against the wall. The rain had stopped and an icy wind was blowing, shaking the walls as it blew the storm toward the north.

An hour later, while everyone else slept, Lilith was still wide awake. She couldn't stop caressing Herlitzka's sewn ankle, running her fingertips over the filament stitches. She sensed in the semidarkness that Yanka was awake, rubbing her belly.

'Are you asleep?' she whispered.

'No.'

Another silence in which Lilith could hear Yanka's restlessness, her head shouting although it barely moved.

'What's the matter?'

'I want to show you something,' Yanka said.

She got up and walked noiselessly over to the fire, where only a few embers remained. She grabbed a small shovel that lay in a pile with other tools and checked to see the others were all sleeping as she came back. The adults were a chorus of snores and her brothers were all arms and legs in the corner as always. Yanka knelt down on the ground in front of her bed, gesturing to Lilith to do the same. With some effort, now that her belly was always in the way, she lay down on her side and slid her body under the cot. She shoved two piles of books aside and felt around in the semidarkness until she found a small patch of loose earth. She didn't have to dig much because the box she was seeking was barely covered by a few shovelfuls of dirt. She brushed the dirt off with her hand.

Lilith watched her wide-eyed without speaking, not understanding what she was doing.

'I have one, too,' Yanka said.

'What?'

'A doll.'

She lifted the lid. Inside, in addition to some papers and a gun, there was a doll the same size as Herlitzka. She had very long black hair, down to her knees. Her face, hands and feet were carved from wood, and she had gigantic black eyes. Her nose was straight and her lips were thick and she had a swollen belly and wore a handwoven tunic…

'What's her name?'

'Wakolda.'

Although her eyes had grown accustomed to the dark, Lilith couldn't make out the details. But something, probably the mystery or the care with which Yanka removed Wakolda from the box and combed her hair with her fingers, made her want to have that doll for herself more than anything in the world.

'Why do you keep her hidden?'

'I don't. It's Cumín.'

'And why does your dad keep her hidden there?'

'He's not my dad.'

The reply made Lilith shut her mouth.

'He says I'm too old for dolls and that I can't have a cloth one if I'm going to have a flesh and blood one.'

'Tell him it's for the baby.'

'I told him and he didn't believe me. He told me he burned it, but Lemún told me he'd buried it here.'

'May I touch her?'

Yanka gave her the doll. The skin was soft and velvety.

'It's incense.'

'What is?'

'The wood. It's pure incense.'

The eyes looked alive, with false eyelashes.

'Can you keep a secret?'

Lilith nodded yes.

'It has powers.'

'What kind of powers?'

'It makes wishes come true. It made my wishes come true.'

'Which ones?'

'I can't tell you… A *machi* made it.'

'A what?'

'A *machi*… You call him – a warlock, a magician.'

Only the extremities were made of wood, and the rest of the body was soft with stuffing. Yanka stuck out an arm and felt along the surface of the cot above their heads until she found one of Herlitzka's hands. She slid it toward her and set her on the ground.

'Would you like to trade?'

Lilith looked at Herlitzka, who was perfect despite the suture, and then at Wakolda, misshapen but powerful. She bit her lip, pretending not to understand, in order to win time.

'What do you mean, trade?'

'I keep yours and you keep mine.'

'Ah… No… Well… It's that…'

'Say it.'

'I don't know.'

'It's to your advantage.'

She looked at one and then the other, but it was impossible for Wakolda not to win out. It was not just her powers. She had come into her hands in the middle of a stormy night at the end of the world, dug up, covered in dirt… Who could resist her? Lilith had a pirate's soul and her mouth watered just thinking about the haul she was making.

'OK, I'll trade with you.'

Like any pirate she would have preferred to trick her at the last minute and end up with both dolls, but Yanka was a worthy adversary. She placed Herlitzka in the box and put the lid on before burying it in the hole. Lilith had a jab of anguish. It was an image she wouldn't forget.

'You're going to leave her there?'

Yanka nodded as she shovelled dirt on top of the box.

'What if he finds her?'

'All the better.'

Yanka had been wanting to get back at Cumín for several months and now, finally… She had no idea what she was doing but she wasn't the sort to stop and think. She acted. Her escapes always took her forward. Her pregnancy was a shield that protected her from being beaten. She knew what awaited her. She'd get yelled at and insulted, shaken up a bit, but nothing she couldn't get over. The satisfaction she felt was tied to the value of what she was turning over to this unsuspecting stranger.

'Hide her well. He can't see her until after you're gone.'

Lilith nodded and wrapped Wakolda in a pink hand-knit blanket she had used for Herlitzka. She hid the wooden legs and all the black curls. The surge of courage had passed and she was seized with regret. She looked at Yanka, who had already lain down again, her dirt-covered hands resting on the seven-month-gone belly.

'Do you feel sorry to have it?'

'No,' Yanka said, closing her eyes.

Lilith fought sleep as best she could. The image of Herlitzka lying buried beneath her body became so unbearable that at one point she was about to get up and free her. But for some reason she didn't. Twelve years old and already true to her word.

* * *

When dawn came and her mother woke her to get back on the road, she looked around without understanding where she was, or who the pregnant girl sleeping beside her was, or the man in the hat sitting at the table who looked at her out of the corner of his eye as he combed his hair, dipping his comb into a glass of water and studying his image in a piece of mirror hanging on the wall. But it was enough for Lilith to make out the eyes of the Mapuche doll looking out from the folds of the blanket for her to immediately remember what had happened. She covered her and yanked a flake of skin from her upper lip, suddenly wide awake with the excitement of some good mischief. She didn't let go of Wakolda during the time it took her parents to get their children up to drink their boiled *maté* and eat the warm pieces of bread Cumín set on the table. That morning, without the trace of alcohol in his blood, he was more tight-lipped than the night before. Fed up with so many people, he wanted them gone. Standing in the outhouse a few yards from the house, now barely a hole in the ground filled with sawdust, Enzo was also anxious to get on the road. He ordered his wife under his breath not to let anyone ask to use the bathroom so they could get on the road immediately. Now that the emergency was over, there was nothing left to share with these people.

'Thanks, Cumín. I don't know how to thank you…'

'That compass would be enough.'

He pointed to Enzo's trouser pocket, from which a silver chain and compass hung, a gift from his brother-in-law.

'Ah, well… If you wish…'

'It was a joke. I don't want a thing.'

'No, take it, please.'

Making an effort to recall the principle of Christian generosity, Enzo undid the compass and put it in the hands of the owner of the house.

'You'll use it more than I will. Take it.'

'All right,' Cumín said without hesitating.

They accompanied the strangers to the overhang under the eaves of the house. Cumín made the mastiff get out of the car before they left and held his dogs at bay while the mastiff ran around helter-skelter peeing on every bush, carried away with territorialism which one of the owner's dogs had sealed with Mapuche urine. Before they got him back into the car though one of the dogs went for his jugular, despite Cumín and his sons trying to kick them apart. The mastiff, now overwhelmed by the chaos into which his domestic life had sunk during the past twenty-four hours, jumped up into the car with bite marks on his neck and back. He nestled between Tomás' legs, resting his snout on his feet and closing his eyes, hoping to get out of there as soon as possible.

'Let's get going, Enzo, please,' Eva begged.

Damp and the worse for wear, even the engine was slow to start. So much so that they all thought they'd have to spend another day there. Tomás held his breath until he heard it start. He felt a stab of pain in the middle of his forehead – proportional to the extent that the brothers had considered slashing him during the night. Lilith, on the other hand, crossed her fingers. Underneath her lace jersey, she was the only adventurous soul. The dryness had returned in all its dusty splendour and there were no evidence on the dried-out ground of the hours of rain. Years of drought had managed to suck up the last drop of rain like a sponge. The only thing that had changed were the colours. With the dust washed away, the bushes were a darker tone of green, the tin of the overhanging roof was shiny and the road was once again black with shimmering mirages every few yards. No one from the house asked them if they had water. They had no intention of sharing their reserves with them. As they watched the car drive off, they said goodbye with a dryness reminiscent of the landscape. The last image Lilith had was of Cumín standing with the compass in his hand, Nahuel and Lemún a few steps behind, with the comic book sticking out of the latter's pocket. One of the drawings of an execution was stuck to his skin. Yanka, as always, stood alone in the doorway, waiting...

5

Twenty miles down the road, Enzo stuck his hand out the window and motioned for José to pull over to the edge of the road. He stopped a prudent distance away. He saw Lilith and her brother run off in different directions to hide behind the tallest bushes they could find. From where he stood he could see Lilith squatting down with her dress pulled up to her waist and her legs spread apart. She had tried to hide behind a bush that was so dry that it didn't take much imagination to complete the outlines of her body. He always felt a particular inclination to study the scatological acts of his specimens. A colleague had called it perverse, but he preferred to believe that those moments, in the grimace of effort or pleasure, were when one could see the essence of the object of study. He could see the details from where he was standing and he could barely make out whether Lilith had her eyes closed or was smiling with relief. What he did see with absolute clarity was the little shaking jig she did before letting her dress back down again to cover her thighs. He saw her give a little jump to avoid the small puddle that she had left at her feet as she ran back to the car, all with the careless enchantment of someone as yet unaware of the mountains her beauty was going to move. Lilith smiled at him before getting back in the car and would have run over to him if it hadn't been for the argument she had had with her parents during the short trip between the cabin and this first stop.

'He isn't a stranger!'

'Yes, he is! He's a stranger. A stranger with whom we happened to spend the night! Nothing more!'

'But…'

'You are not going to ride with him in his car, Lilith,' Eva said without raising her voice.

It was the tone that preceded punishment and so she shut her mouth and occupied herself with looking out of the window. Her father breathed heavily, his neck full of sweat and his skin various shades darker than usual… And they still had over 600 miles to go, half of it without tarmac. Lilith remembered with absolute clarity the exasperation they all felt last summer during the last hundred miles of the trip. They couldn't stand to talk to or touch each other and any contact with her brothers caused a fight. She saw a truck in the distance that was pulling away from a cabin with five men in back. Lilith imagined it was the same truck that picked Cumín and his sons up for another workday.

'Here's where it ends,' the father said with resignation.

What was ending was the tarmac. You could see in the distance the break where the road turned once more into dirt and rubble. A few miles later she felt the swaying in her body the moment that the wheels passed from one texture to another, the line between what the country was going to be and what it was. Deafened by a concert of sounds, Lilith hugged Wakolda against her body and closed her eyes. The creaking of metal was met by the louder and louder panting of the mastiff, who drooled in the corner, gasping for air, and the crying of her younger brother, for whom 600 miles was an infinite distance. She rolled down the window a few inches and raised her nose toward the hot and humid air, letting her hair whip around her and hiding her face so no one could see her tears.

'Every family has someone who's crazy and someone who cries,' her grandmother had told her the last time she saw her.

'I'm the one who gets to be crazy and you're the one who gets to cry.'

Lilith nodded. She didn't speak German, but she understood it. Eva had spoken the language of her childhood when she raised them. She didn't even remember why she cried that night, but the lullaby her grandmother sang her to sleep with was carved in her mind:

Schlaf, Kindlein, schlaf!
Der Vater hüt' die Schaf,
Die Mutter schüttelt 's Bäumelein,
Da fähllt herab ein Träumelein.
Schlaf, Kindlein, schlaf!

'The meaning doesn't matter,' her grandmother would say. 'Just listen to the music.'

The only thing Lilith couldn't understand were the arguments between her grandmother and her mother. They spoke so rapidly that the words turned into a roar filled with Rs. Her grandmother barely got out of bed that last summer, having abandoned her body as she had the house and the garden. She'd been begging them for years to move to the south, but Eva refused to do so with the same vehemence with which the grandmother insisted on it.

'I'm going to have to die for you to come back here,' she said.

That's what had happened.

Enzo gathered his family together in early December to tell them that they were not going to go back to school the next year in Buenos Aires because they were moving to the south. He had spent the morning packing into boxes the tools from his workbench, on which were placed dozens of watches of all sizes. Lulled by the infinite division of time of a hundred watches, each one beating with its own rhythm, his workbench was the only place Enzo relaxed. In a corner far enough removed so as not to upset Eva, he kept his porcelain containers, his brushes, the mould and the small oven where he fired some dolls during his spare time. But every day the ratio got a little more messed up. Enzo spent his afternoons working on the outlines of a lip, a pair of eyebrows, a mole right on the tip of the mouth, inserting glass eyes, finishing up a nylon shell with a tiny linen wig, rubbing the skin of the porcelain bodies until they felt as soft as a newborn… Hours and hours, instead of finishing up the watches he had to repair. His final invention, which meant inserting a watch in place of the heart, had captured his imagination with such fury that he ate his latest meals in silence, tracing a mechanism in his food that would fasten the watch in the inside of the porcelain bodies. Eva knew well where his mind was every time he stared at her blankly. Those dolls, that barely allowed her husband to sleep, produced in her attacks of jealousy that were stronger than those of any flesh and blood woman Enzo might have got involved with. Lilith had heard them argue hundreds of times…

'No one can make a living from those dolls! And even less from fixing bearings and motors! Not even if all the watches in Buenos Aires broke at the same time!'

'In that case we'd become millionaires,' Enzo replied the night before his announcement, with his usual calmness.

Eva said nothing, but the next day Lilith's father announced to them that they were going to reopen his in-laws' guesthouse. His work made barely enough to feed them. He did not confess to them that they had reached an agreement: if they could find something else to keep them afloat, Eva would leave him and his dolls alone. Lilith didn't dare complain. She knew that if their mother stood staring silently at the ground it was because there was no going back. Her father was nothing more than the messenger of a decision she had taken on her own.

'Wake up, Lilith… We're here.'

She opened her eyes in the middle of the darkness of a poorly lit street. She was carsick, dizzy, all sticky and dirty, like they all were. Each one of her muscles hurt, even those she hadn't known existed. José, with his training as a soldier, had stood the road trip better than any of them. But his eyes burned and he had a throbbing pain in his forehead. They had left the desert behind as the sun had set and the first trees appeared around a bend in the road, along with streams that got wider and wider as they nourished the land, turning it into the oasis they had promised him. When darkness had overtaken the landscape, he had glued his eyes to the car he had been following forever, with no other thought than to stay awake until they stopped.

Now that they had reached the end of the trip, he could just about see, half hidden by the forests of the Andean range, an Alpine-style chalet. They were only about a hundred yards from the largest lake in Patagonia. He had no idea about his next step, but a suitcase replete with Swiss francs would be enough to keep him calm. Enzo was already coming over to the car of the stranger who had followed them over the course of more than 600 miles. He was walking with a slight limp in his left leg, cramped after ten hours of pressing down on the accelerator.

José got out of the car.

The wind coming down off Nahuel Huapi caught him off guard, hitting him fully with a cold, dry blast. He saw Tomás undoing the lock on an iron gate before pushing it open with Lilith's help. The windows of the chalet were lit up and in the light they cast around them he could make out the opulence in stone and wood of a bygone era.

'We're stopping here, José. Bariloche is a dozen miles further ahead, straight down this same road… In which direction are you going?'

José took a piece of paper folded in the middle from the inside pocket of his jacket. Enzo read the address and looked up, nodding.

'Are these friends of yours?' he asked.

'Acquaintances.'

'It's in town. Keeping going straight and ask again once you get there. Anyone can tell you where it is.'

José nodded without saying a word. Behind Enzo, he saw Eva walking with the children down a road lined with pine trees that end at a house. The confusion he felt since his exile, the loss of meaning, the hopelessness… all suddenly evaporated. He was not going to miss the opportunity to live in that zoo.

'Your daughter was telling me you plan on reopening your in-laws' guesthouse.'

On the verge of saying goodbye, Enzo looked at him surprised. He had no idea when he had shared so much information with his daughter.

'In a few weeks.'

'If that's true, I could be your first guest. I and my wife.'

Like a good Christian, José knew that marriage was a synonym of tranquility. Renting to a single man was not the same thing as renting to a sacred institution.

'The idea is to send for her as soon as I have settled down somewhere.'

'You're married?'

'Of course.'

'Let me talk to my wife. If she agrees, perhaps we could rent you one of the ground-floor rooms. Of course, only if you like it…'

'I'll like it.'

Enzo shook hands with him, concluding the conversation. He needed to be patient. It was clear they were worn out by the trip. The only one to turn around to wave at him was Lilith, with the Mapuche doll hidden in a wool blanket clutched close to her body. The rest of the family seemed to have forgotten him. They couldn't stand being cooped up in the car any more and wanted to stretch their legs.

'Come see us tomorrow.'

'Around noon?'

'Better in the afternoon. Five o'clock.'

Lilith heard the motor of the Chevrolet as it pulled away. She would have run off to catch up with it if she hadn't been imprisoned in Luned's arms – a Welshwoman full of freckles who had worked for her grandmother since the time Lilith learned to walk. She was as decrepit as the house and had not slept for the past two nights waiting for them. Seated on one of the stone lions that decorated the entrance, her daughter Tegai was also waiting for them. She smiled at them with her crooked teeth. Her body seemed to have undergone an explosion of curves since last summer, so much so that Tomás could barely make out the line of her jaw. The two Welshwomen had used up the last of the pile of wood keeping the house warm for them. They had started to go crazy, talking to the echo of their own words in the deserted halls of the house, when Eva informed them that they were travelling south to live there.

Lilith was the only one who dared enter the main bedroom that night. The only one to ask how it had happened.

'In her sleep.'

'Right here?'

'In this very bed. Your grandmother always got her way.'

An ancient dollhouse was waiting for her at the side of the bed. It shone inside and out, once the spiderwebs and insects had been cleared from its corners. Lilith had never seen anything like it before. She looked in at the windows of the ground floor with her (giant) eyes. The first thing she saw was a tiny grand piano, the rest of the furniture was just as magical…

'I found it in the attic when I was sorting some things,' Tegai said. 'It belonged to your mother. Your grandmother told me to clean it up for you.'

She didn't dare touch that miniature world, so tidy it made her afraid. Lilith slept in that same room, holding Wakolda tight. The sheets had no trace of her grandmother's smell. They smelled of the white soap the Welshwomen had used to scrub them with over and over again until they had removed death from each silk thread. The sound of the motor of a hydroplane woke her up a few minutes after dawn. It was the second time she had woken up to find the world around her had changed form. The Mapuche doll, which she clutched like an anchor, once again oriented her… She jumped out of bed, put on her wellies and, leaping down the stairs like a gazelle, ran over to the large windows that overlooked the garden. It had been one of her favourite pastimes the past few summers, running toward the dock each time they were alerted by the sound of an engine flying over the house. Sometimes weeks would go by with no landing, and she wasn't about to lose out on the chance that someone had come to welcome them. She brushed the branches away from her face as she ran through tall grass and fallen trunks and across the 300 yards that sloped down to the lake shore. By the time she reached the dock, a hydroplane was flying over the lake, about to hit the water. Tomás had beaten her by a few seconds. There was a tiny cut on his forehead from a branch or thorn and a small drop of blood ran down his brow, although he wasn't aware of it.

'Eight, seven, six, five, four…,' he counted, out of breath.

Lilith joined his countdown, saying the last three numbers faster so that the zero corresponded to the smack of the hydroplane as it hit the water so gently that it barely broke the surface before gliding toward the neighbouring dock. The house that belonged to the dock was some 200 yards away, at the foot of a mountain. It could barely be seen from the road and the entrance was no more than a trace of dirt along one of the many turn-offs hidden by the thickness of the forest. Unless you knew about it you'd barely see it if you were coming by land. The easiest ways to get there were by air or water and the hydroplane was the perfect combination. Her grandmother had once told her that the widow of the owner, a Swiss man who was one of the first settlers in the city, had sold it to an outsider several months after his death. The city was growing in leaps and bounds at that stage and every day more and more people came to Bariloche to start a new life. One of the favourite pastimes of the long-time residents was to gather information about the newcomers. But they had only seen the owner of the neighbouring house a handful of times and knew nothing about him. From where she stood, shivering in her night clothes, Lilith managed to glimpse fleetingly a man wearing dark glasses and a woman in a broad-brimmed hat sitting in the back behind the pilot. It was usually the only glimpse they had of the visitors before the hydroplanes disappeared under the grape-laden bower that became thicker closer in to the house.

'Are there still a lot of people arriving?' Lilith asked, still upset.

'All the time,' Tegai whispered. 'More and more each time.'

They stood stock-still without talking so they could hear the motor as it shut down, the creaking of an iron gate shutting and the barking of a couple of dogs as they received the new arrivals. All they knew about the neighbour was that he received visitors who never left the house. Anything else that happened there was a secret hidden behind the fifteen-foot high walls that surrounded the property, along with the poplars and eucalyptuses that hid the house.

That very afternoon, with Tomás' help, they set a ladder against the tallest pine of the dividing wall that separated them from the neighbouring property and climbed up until they reached a branch that allowed them to see a portion of the grounds that surrounded the next-door house. Lying face down on the largest branches, half hidden by the leaves, the eldest two were more focused on their own excitement than in seeing what was going on on the other side. Tomás picked a twig and used it to raise Tegai's skirt. Pretending she didn't see him, the Welsh girl waited to see what he was up to before shooing him away with a kick. Lilith was the only one paying attention, but she still couldn't see a thing. The windows in the distance were strategically hidden behind the trees. They refused to give up and stood guard for more than an hour. Their perseverance yielded results. At that magic hour when the light makes everything seem lovelier than it is, they saw a man walking among the trees. His forehead, nose and chin were bandaged and he looked more like a mummy than a man. He moved slowly, as if he were still under anaesthesia.

Lilith wasn't able to stay hidden. She couldn't stop looking at him, even though they were only a few yards apart. She didn't lower her head when Tomás whispered to her to do so. The man must have sensed he was being observed, because he turned and saw her there sitting on a branch. She could have sworn he smiled at her, although his bottom lip was also half hidden beneath a bandage. Lilith was on the verge of losing her balance and landing flat on her back on the ground. She stifled a scream and scrambled down from branch to branch in such a hurry that she slipped two yards from the ground and fell on her knees, splitting them both open. Tegai and Tomás jumped down behind her, laughing as they galloped toward the trees surrounding the guesthouse. They were quicker than she was, and in a matter of seconds she fell a few yards behind them. She managed to see Tomás grabbed Tegai by the waist to make her disappear behind a tree. She heard laughter, but she quickly lost them from view.

All upset, she stopped to look for them.

'Tegai?'

No one answered.

Their laughter sound far off and muffled, someone's mouth stifling the other's. She knew what they were doing and it infuriated her that they left her out of their games. She ran a few yards more, still bothered by the image of the bandaged man. She stopped when she saw the German's car, which was parked on the other side of a thick maleberry hedge. As she approached, she saw José adjusting his hat with the concentration of a film star. When he saw her, he got out of the car and walked towards her without taking his eyes off her. He had two bottles of wine, a bouquet of flowers and his pockets were full of sweets he planned to give to the youngest brother just as he had done for years with the ones he selected. Those pockets full of sugar that brought so much happiness were the best bait.

'This is for you,' he said, plucking a daisy from the bouquet.

In no hurry and taking his time so he wouldn't crush a single petal, he wove it through the squares of the wire fence. Lilith bit her lip, her gaze fixed on the orange-coloured center of the flower.

'Is your father home?'

Lilith whispered yes, barely a tickle on her tongue. She'd never felt so unsettled in the presence of a man... She handled like no one else the art of provocation and irreverence. Timidity, on the other hand, was a new feeling for her. José waited five seconds, more patient than ever before.

'Go find him,' he ordered, exasperated after six seconds.

Lilith turned and ran toward the house. The night before, lying in her mother's lap as she had her hair caressed, she had listened to her parents speaking in German. Her father was the most reluctant about having a stranger come to live with them before they'd even opened the guesthouse.

'We don't know him...'

'We're not going to know any of the people who stay here,' Eva said, who had grown up surrounded by strangers. 'That's not the idea. They're paying guests, not friends. If we fix up one of the rooms on the left wing we won't even have to see him much...'

Her father didn't take him right away, but they spent the next day cleaning the house. He had agreed to return on the condition that everyone would help him transform the house. He wanted no more locked doors. He had a locksmith come out from the town to open more than a dozen locks for which there were no keys. Years of dust and cobwebs had turned the rooms into stuffy abandoned attics filled with insects and rodent droppings. But there was something else. In the silence and darkness of those rooms something had slowly fermented that gripped them like the hand of an invisible giant now calling out to be exorcised. Luned brought along two of her sisters and a couple of cousins to wage the war. Armed with rags and buckets of soapy water, they set out like an army of bulldozers, opening shutters and windows before them. Enzo and Tomás undertook to take outside the furniture that could still be salvaged and they lost no time in sanding history away from every surface. Lilith's job was to take the old clothes that had been rotting away for years in drawers and closets down to the washroom on the first floor, and she was busy with that when she found her mother sitting in one of the rooms that had been already cleared out by the Welsh Amazons. Sitting with the sun on her face, Eva was going through a box filled with old photos, school notebooks and children's reading books.

'I don't know why your grandmother did this…'

She pointed to the dozens of boxes piled up against the wall.

'She put everything away in the rooms in unmarked boxes. When one room became full of old things, she locked it and proceeded to lose the key. After I left for Buenos Aires, I would always have the same nightmare. Your father and I would buy a house that seemed very airy, but when we walk through it I start to find unfamiliar new rooms, halls and rooms that get darker and dirtier… I always end up in an immense open space, like a barn or sometimes a stage that's part of the house and where anyone can walk in. In some of my dreams, the doors lead to alleys or terraces. Last night I dreamt the house was full of strangers. I fed them and took care of them, afraid to tell them I wanted them to leave. I created meals using the last remnants of the cupboards: sausages, fruit, vegetables.

The people invaded the house, going into the rooms they shouldn't, muddying the floors and dirtying the bathrooms. Finally I stopped the music and gathered them together to tell them my mother was dying and they had to leave. Now I want to fill this house with people... I think I'm turning it into the house of my nightmares.'

She had never heard her mother talk so much, out of breath, as though talking in a confidential tone to a friend. For once in her life, Lilith didn't say a word.

'Look,' Eva said, holding a photograph in her hand. 'That's me.'

She pointed to a little girl with braids in a uniform. In the photograph, a group of fifty children were smiling as they sat in front of the door of a pitched-roof schoolhouse, next to a sign that Lilith read:

PRIMO CAPRARO SCHOOL

Many of them held their arm out in front of them. The Argentine flag was to one side and on the other there was a red flag with a swastika.

'Does your school still exist?'

'They closed it during the war. They reopened it two years ago. Many of those in the photograph are going to be your teachers.'

'That's where I'm going to go?'

'Yes.'

'But I don't speak German.'

'That's not important. They have two groups. One of them is taught in Spanish.'

'Did Dad go there too?'

'You father's not German.'

'Neither am I.'

Lilith pawed through the photographs until she found one of the few in which there was a group picture with her grandparents. Her father was the only one who was not smiling. When she looked up she saw her mother frowning at her, as if her face had some memory written on it.

'One day your father told them his children were Argentine and that they should speak the language of the country with you.'

'What happened?'

'They kicked us out.'

'All of us?'

'Your father. They told me to choose.'

Eva put the photos and notebooks back in the box.

'And…' Lilith murmured.

'I left with him.'

A thousand things were going through Lilith's head, but she only stammered, 'Wow.'

She could barely contain herself, swinging her feet back and forth and to the side. She looked at her mother with fresh eyes and saw in her a courageous warrior. Now she understood everything: the disdain with which her grandparents had treated Enzo for years, Eva's reluctance to spend summers with them, the tense calm of the three weeks they'd spend under the same roof with them every year. Before sending her off to take a bath, Eva asked her not to mention the story to anyone.

'This is between you and me, understood?'

Lilith swore herself to silence and managed to keep quiet for about an hour before she told Tomás and Tegai as they dragged the ladder toward the neighbour's hedge. She would have told the German too, so entranced was she by the story, but they never left them alone together. Her father received

76

him at the front door and led him to the parlour. The house was clean and fresh inside and the smell of a roast in the oven came from the kitchen. Tomás had just placed some wood on the fire in the grate. José was in such good humour that, even though he was a vegetarian, the aroma of the cooking meat whet his appetite. He patted Tomás on the head and went to look out the large windows facing the lake... The place was a paradise.

'*Wilkommen*,' Eva said.

She blushed and closed her mouth. It brought so many memories to be in the house of her childhood and she was surprised to find herself speaking the language she had been brought up speaking. She gave the bouquet of flowers to Tegai and served some tea, while José smiled as he examined the room. A short call to the capital last night had been enough for a network of local contacts to swing immediately into action. Everyone offered to open their homes up to him while he decided whether to carry on or to remain for a while in Bariloche. José turned all the offers down without any explanation and he didn't even bother to tell a colleague who was waiting for him with the table ready that he wasn't going to sleep at his house. He spent the night in a hotel in town and had dinner with a bunch of noisy tourists, locking himself in his room before 10 p.m. His survival instinct advised him not to contact anyone until he had decided what he was going to do. He had no intention of explaining why he preferred to pay to live with strangers when it would have been an honour for so many people to have him as a guest.

'You know how I feel?' he said to Enzo. 'Like I've come home.'

He went over to Eva to take the cup of tea she offered him. Overly perfumed and shaven so his skin glowed fresh, he wore a black suit, newly shined shoes and the hat he'd had on yesterday… He was the image of fastidiousness. He could see himself living in a place like this.

'And the lake!' he exclaimed. 'How good that lake makes me feel!'

Eva smiled. She felt the same way.

'I was describing it to my wife on the phone yesterday,' José said in German, as he thrust a silver spoon into the sugar bowl.

'And when might she be coming?' Eva asked.

Enzo's glance made her repeat the question, now in Spanish. 'When might she be coming?'

'As soon as I get settled somewhere.'

He looked at Lilith's parents, as if it was up to them to make an announcement to him. Enzo and Eva glanced at each other, confused by a new direction in the zig-zagging conversation.

'I don't know if you've made up your mind…'

'The guesthouse won't be ready for two weeks.'

'All I need is a room with a view like this.'

'Didn't you have somewhere to stay?' Enzo asked, still reluctant.

José took advantage of the pause to push his advantage.

'I've been looking at hotels, boarding houses, apartments to rent. Nothing seems as welcoming to me as this house. All I want is a nice home for my wife… Our life has been so difficult these last few months and we need some peace and quiet. I'm prepared to pay whatever's necessary to get it. Money's not a problem. I can pay in advance. Six months.'

Without any hesitation, he took a stack of Argentine pesos from his pocket and set it on the table. He pushed it toward Enzo with the tip of his finger. Eva took a sip of tea, her eyes glued to the bills. Without counting it, she knew that it was enough to pay the debts from the last months and live on for a couple of weeks until the guesthouse was up and running. Lilith held her breath as she looked at her mother. Eva nodded, giving in to her nightmare.

'Tell your wife to come,' she said.

José treated them all to one of his frosty smiles.

'It's an honour for me to be the first guest.'

'Do you have any luggage?'

'In the car.'

'I'll go get it,' Enzo said.

Eva put the money away and stood up to show him the way.

'Follow me,' she said in German. 'I'll show you your room.'

Although the heat of the fire burned Lilith's legs, she couldn't move. She wanted to shout with joy. She saw them climb the stairs and turn toward the wing reserved for guests. She had to restrain herself so as not to follow them, almost wagging her tail like a happy puppy. José took advantage of the few yards along the dark passage to examine Eva's body, fascinated by that combination of gravity and sensuality of pregnant women.

'May I ask you something?'

Eva nodded without stopping.

'Are you certain you're eighteen weeks along?

'That's what the doctor said.'

'You're too large… Were they all as big?'

'Tomás and the youngest.'

'And Lilith,' José asked.

'She was born two months premature.'

She stopped in front of one of the cedar doors and opened it. José stuck his head inside to have a look. It was a small room with a single bed and a desk with a view of the lake. He walked around the room with a smile, stopping to open the windows to breathe with his eyes closed.

'Perfect.'

Eva smiled, standing in the doorway.

'Were you raised here?' José asked her.

'*I was born here.*'

Something in the German's look made her uncomfortable. So much so she put the room key down on the desk.

'Your key. We'll have the dining room set up again for guests tomorrow. You can eat with us today.'

It was the only stipulation she'd made to Enzo: she refused to share her meals with a stranger. Not even for the two weeks it would take them to reopen the doors of the guesthouse. They had to remain as independent as possible, just as they had when Eva was a child, when her parents' house was divided in two parts. They lived on one side and the guests on the other. That night, José made a superhuman effort to swallow the tripe stew they placed before him. The gummy nature of the meat he was chewing made him gag more than once. He hid it with a dry cough behind a handkerchief with his initials on it. Vegetarianism was an eccentricity in this part of the world and he wasn't going to disdain their food the first night. He stayed calm and quiet during the meal, answering politely but without going into details on any topic. On the contrary, he took refuge in questions designed to uncover the genealogy of both parents in search of something that would allow him to understand the diversity of their offspring. He learned that Lilith had had pneumonia when she was three and she still suffered from a light case of asthma. It was normal for her to have colds, headaches, respiratory infections and sinusitis. Tomás and the youngest, on the other hand, never got sick. Lilith was flattered that he wanted to know everything about her, how much she weighed, how tall she was…

'Four foot three,' her mother said.

'Four foot four,' she said, with the precision of a star pupil.

The German smiled, wiping his mouth with the napkin as he turned to look at Eva.

'How much did she weigh?'

'Aren't you a veterinarian?'

José glanced around at his small accomplice. He would have liked to ask her how much else she'd told them.

'Doctor. Veterinarian. Anthropologist.'

'And which do you prefer... Humans or animals?'

'They're about the same, aren't they?'

He followed his joke with a sip of wine. Eva and Enzo exchanged glances, intimidated by his recital of university degrees.

'What is your specialty?'

'Cattle. Few people realise how much you can increase the number of births and improve breeds through hormones.'

'What kind of hormones?'

'Ones for growth.'

'One cow at a time?' Lilith murmured.

'Only pregnant ones. You stimulate their production of a protein the body produces naturally, but in small doses. Genetics is a complex science, but there are simple explanations. What is most important is always looking for what geneticists call *the founding effect*. If you can find a clear hereditary pattern, you can work to improve the breed.'

'Do you plan on working on that while you're here?'

'Probably.'

Glancing at Eva's belly, José was on the point of saying that if his clinical judgement wasn't off – he'd calculated the weeks remaining just by touch – she had less time remaining than she thought. But if his intuition was correct, there was something else... The idea whet his appetite, as he had not seen twins since the war. Digestion was slow and painful, as his body was only used to greens, milk products and legumes. He sank into a profound dream that took him back to the Führer. He was in a dark underground corridor. He lived there, buried alive. His moustache was long, as in some First World War photographs. José shouted after him when he saw him turning on his heels to walk away, begging him not to leave. He swore he'd follow him anywhere, even those places he didn't believe in, like the secret cities of the Himalayas or the subterranean hideouts in Antarctica… The Führer turned his back on him and walked away alone, without looking back at him once.

He awoke, unable to breathe.

There were many who said that the General had not died in his bunker and that he'd left by submarine and was now holed up in one of his polar oases. Like Barbarossa, King Arthur, Baldur and Wotan, dead and undead, alive and not alive, frozen, hibernating, while crows watched over his dreams, to awaken him when the Aryan race would need them again. People said the war was not over, that it would never end. But José was a man of science and he didn't believe in magic, alchemy or any kind of hermeticism. He didn't believe in magic mountains or secret cities in which, as people said, the survivors had taken refuge. He was convinced that the destiny of man would only be solved above ground. For the first time in months he had to take one of the tranquilisers which he used to put out the patients who on a handful of occasions had awakened in him an unexpected gesture of pity.

6

Lilith entered José's room through the window and walked around his bed with a smile. She knew the house by heart. Her grandmother had shown her all the passageways and short-cuts. She knew the basement was connected to the laundry by a system of tunnels that had been sealed off thirty feet in the direction of the neighbours by a cave-in no one had bothered to fix. During one of her escapades she had discovered that the gutters of the roof were wide enough to walk on without falling. This allowed her access to all the rooms, even the ones that were locked. The locks were so old that whoever had the key took a while to get the door open. The rattling of the key in the lock gave her enough time to run to the window and vanish. She moved around like a ghost, and no one had any secrets from her. She made sure that, before escaping through the window of the room, she had enough time to examine whatever she wanted: the flamboyant guest and her father were discussing details of his stay in the dining room. José had been surprised that morning to find he was being served breakfast in the sitting room of the left wing, with a view of the forest, while the rest of the family ate in the right-wing dining room, facing Nahuel Huapi. His surprise was even greater when Luned gave him a set of keys so he could come and go by the side door that led to that same room. Under such conditions he would go days without bumping into Lilith and her family. The gesture seemed a concern for his privacy, but nothing could have been further from what he had imagined, which was to follow the progress of Eva's pregnancy and the growth of her three children…

What was the purpose? he asked himself,
Why did he take notes like crazy? he had no idea.

For right now it was nothing more than a diversion to overcome his outrage at having to flee the comfort of his home in Buenos Aires with no promise that his life would return to normality.

She opened the top of the desk in José's room and leaned over to look inside without touching a thing. A silver ring caught her attention. It had a skull and some other symbols she didn't recognise, not identifying the swastika or the runic writing. She moved it a few inches with the tip of the index finger. It had an inscription in German on the inside. She tried it on, even though she knew it was too large for fingers as tiny as hers. She saw a dagger in a leather shield resting on top of a black notebook. She carefully withdrew it, and the slight trembling of her hands sprinkled the walls of the room with flashes of light. The stranger was becoming more and more fascinating to her. The metal gleamed and each one of its sides had another engraved emblem she wasn't able to make out. More and more intrigued and having forgotten by then that she was going through someone else's belongings, she opened the notebook. Pages and pages of notes, numbers, lists, drawings. It was filled with illustrations of children and babies with arrows coming from their eyes, heads, extremities and organs. On one of the pages she saw two bodies joined at the back. When she got to the end she stopped short. Her mother was the first one she recognised, naked and seven months pregnant. It wasn't a particularly good drawing, but close enough for there to be no doubt in her mind it was her. There was a series of numbers scattered around her: measurements, estimated weight, number of months pregnant.

Homo arabicus, she read.

Her father occupied the following page, alongside her brothers, also surrounded by numbers and measurements.

She read: *Homo siriacus*.

She came last.

Her illustration had more details than the others: measurements of almost all her bones, the circumference of her head, notations in German, numbers and more numbers, calculations along with results, a list of illnesses… Feeling a lump in the pit of her stomach, she gathered up the arms and legs of her doll. She left the dagger, the ring and the notebook where she'd found them. She climbed out the window after making sure that everything was exactly as she'd found it.

Back in her room, she sat down on the window ledge. She felt her head spinning and it wasn't because of the height. If she talked, the questions would begin.

How'd you find the notebook?

How'd you get in the room?

Then she'd be punished, a whole month grounded. But what was worse, they'd probably ask the stranger to leave. What difference did it make if he was a doctor, a veterinarian or an anthropologist? Who wanted to be studied? Besides, they weren't animals. And he'd said his specialty was cows. Even if they had to return the money they had already used to pay the last months' debts, they were going to ask him to leave. For once in her life she was going to have to keep her mouth shut. That's what she did, even though she'd never look at him the same way again.

They barely saw each other in the following days.

José knew they were testing to see if they could live with a stranger and he didn't want to do anything to change their opinion. He ate alone, used the side door and changed his course when he saw Eva watering the flowers with Lilith, whom he could see that day was distant, upset and skittish.

They greeted him but kept their distance.

It was midday when Enzo crossed over to the left wing of the house to ask him if everything was all right. He found him sitting on the balcony overlooking the lake, reading a newspaper. Minutes before, in a box buried on page fifteen, José had found a news item taking up less than a quarter of a page, with the headline MOSSAD SEARCHES FOR MENGELE and in smaller type *Sources confirm that the Nazi scientist is likely to already be in Paraguay*. He pretended to read, although he was entertaining himself with the spectacle of the half-naked bodies of Eva and her children. They had plucked up their courage to go swimming in the freezing waters of Nahuel Huapi. When Lilith emerged from the water, he lowered his newspaper to watch her without any pretence. Her body was less deformed than it appeared to be with clothes on. Her legs were short, or her trunk was too long, but there was a mysterious harmony in the imperfection of her measurements. She ran toward Tomás and Tegai, who were playing on the beach with a pair of wooden stilts. They were trying to make the youngest of the children walk on the stilts like a circus monkey.

'Were you looking for me?'

Enzo's voice surprised him with his guard down. Without moving, he shifted the newspaper up a few inches, blocking Lilith from his line of vision before turning around.

'I've obtained the vitamins and iron for your wife's anaemia.'

He took two pill bottles from his case, which Enzo, surprised, took. He had agreed to Eva giving a blood sample to see if she was anaemic. The result was positive. José took it upon himself to prescribe a course of vitamins for her and an iron compound.

'She'll feel better after taking this for a few days.'

'I didn't know you'd…'

'She told me she was tired. I took it upon myself.'

'You shouldn't have bothered.'

José shook his hand, which settled the matter. An outburst of laughter from Lilith, who was trying to stand up on the stilts, made them look up in her direction.

'Did they ever run tests to see if there's still time for her?'

'Time for her for what?' Enzo asked.

'To grow.'

'That's not something medicine decides, is it?'

José smiled, about to launch into one of his favourite areas.

'There are treatments that, if undertaken in time, could push Lilith toward a height that's almost normal. Let me show you something.'

He took a stack of photos from a manila envelope. They had to do with some of his most recent experiments on a couple of ranches on the outskirts of Buenos Aires. A calf that was sickly before receiving his hormone treatment could be seen in the picture of health in the next one.

'This is what my treatment can do.'

'Is it the same animal?'

He nodded.

'There's a month's difference between the photographs.'

He knew it was better not to press the issue, but he couldn't help himself…

'If you'd let me treat Lilith during…'

'A calf's one thing and my daughter's something else,' Enzo interrupted him.

It was the cue he was waiting for to take out older photographs. Children in white tunics, before and after receiving hormones and dietary supplements. Although they were smiling, something in their eyes disturbed Enzo.

'What's this?'

'My patients,' José said, with the impunity still provided by the veil of secrecy that surrounded everything that had gone on during those years. 'The same medications are used on animals and humans…'

He refrained from saying that, by virtue of being chosen those children had been allowed to eat again. They slept in a ward in which they had blankets and could have a bath twice a week and eat three times a day. They looked into the camera as they stood next to a cross on the wall that marked each one's growth curve.

'She could grow something like three inches. Maybe more. All you have to do is allow me to give her a daily injection. There's no more danger than a slight reaction… Why don't you discuss it with Eva and Lilith at least?'

'There's nothing to discuss.'

The evident irritation in his voice caused José to shut his mouth.

'When is your wife arriving?'

'Soon,' he lied.

He said he'd already contacted her and she was packing for the trip. She had to take care of some matters in Buenos Aires first. The truth was he hadn't called her nor had he any intention of doing so. He had no doubt the bloodhounds had her under surveillance and he was not about to allow her to lead them to his hideout. Enzo left without giving him time to ask another question. Just as he was about to shout after him that he wasn't done with him yet, he remembered that he was not one of his subordinates. He cursed himself. He had sworn that he would stop engaging in interrogations, but he found it impossible. He could barely engage in a conversation with members of the inferior races without treating them as subordinates. That's all he had done for years. Almost all of them answered him with total passivity and without looking him in the eye, either too weak or too terrified to show their faces. Only a few, those who knew there was no hope left for them, dared to insult him.

Even though he hadn't given anyone his address, he had already received that day three invitations from colleagues who were in the city in situations similar to his own. They invited him for lunch, for dinner, to receptions for the arrival or the departure of someone or other, on hunting or fishing trips… Social life in Bariloche was active and prosperous and they all assured him that with a minimum of discretion he could live there as long as he wanted without having to worry. They offered to get him an office in a lab so he could continue with his research and a doctor's office if he wanted to go back into practice. José turned down all invitations and offers from his colleagues. He said he still wasn't sure how long he was going to stay. Although he felt strangely at home, he knew the logical thing to do was to prepare to flee to a neighbouring country. How long would it take for the rumour he was hiding out in the south to get through or to reach the wrong person?

'Years,' they told him with complete confidence.

Hardly any news of the outside world reached them in that small tourist town of 8000 inhabitants whose lives mainly revolved around skiing. New arrivals were received with open arms and as Europeans they enjoyed privileged status. The original immigrants had received the new arrivals with no questions asked about their past. The Argentine population wasn't interested in the past of German immigrants either. To kill time, that was all there was right now for him to kill. Yet he still kept, for nostalgia's sake, the small silver chain he used to motion to the left or the right, indicating to the guards in which direction each prisoner was to be led. José decided to take a long walk to Bariloche to meet some friends. He wanted to know what was going on in Buenos Aires. He knew the Federal Police had sent a communiqué to the media with the order for his arrest. There was an offer from Europe of 20,000 Deutschmarks. An employee of the German Embassy in Asunción swore she'd seen him in Colonia Independencia. A CIA rumor had him in hiding in Mato Grosso. Anonymous reports poured in, that he had married a woman in Córdoba, that he was married to someone else, who was wealthy, in Santiago del Estero, that they'd seen him getting on a bus in Corumbá, vaccinating cattle in the frontier towns of Chiloé and Poços de Caldos, disappearing into the crowd on a pedestrian bridge between Clorinda and Namawa... Delighted to be heading toward becoming the stuff of myth, he tucked his gun inside a gabardine jacket, after making sure he was carrying his only indispensable companion, a cyanide capsule, hidden in his shirt pocket. He had practised dozens of times how many seconds it took him to put it in his mouth. Every day he did it faster.

'Will I see you again, Uncle Fritz?' his son had asked.

'Soon,' José lied.

The sharpness of the memory startled him in the middle of the tree-lined and fresh-smelling road to Bariloche, although sometimes months went by without his remembering him. He could hear the rustling of the wind on the water of the lake, mixed with the song of various kinds of birds. He imitated the melody of a swarm of larks. He breathed deeply, cleaning the depths of his lungs with air that hadn't a trace of pollution. He imagined briefly how many people would be willing to kill him if they knew he was living such a peaceful existence.

He couldn't know then that he'd be a fugitive forever, with not a moment's peace until he died. Nor that throughout the coming years he was going to be hunted throughout Latin America, the chase always nipping at his heels… The first time, it was a commando force made up of Auschwitz survivors, in a hotel on the border where the three countries came together. The second time was in the Alto Paraná jungle, at the hands of an adventurer who spent his time assassinating Nazis during the postwar years. It was even harder for him to imagine that he was destined to die penniless and alone, drowning on a beach in Betioga near São Paulo, nor that his remains, not much more than a skull, seven dental fragments and a couple of bones, would be dug up and sent to a medical institute in São Paulo.

The only thing he could count on was that if they found him, they were not going to give him a quick death. He banished his fears when he saw Lilith and Tomás riding their bikes about a half mile from their house. They were peddling standing up and yelling like savages. They were going faster and faster because it was downhill to their house. Lilith slowed her pace when she saw him. She let her brother shoot on ahead and in a few moments they were standing face to face.

'Where's your car?' Lilith asked.

'I wanted to walk.'

Lilith kicked a small stone that shot off in the direction of the lake. She was different, timid, and she'd lost her nerviness. José shifted his gaze to the bandages on her knees.

'Does it hurt?' he asked.

'A little bit.'

'Don't do that again.'

'Climb up on something?'

'Spy,' he said, without explaining how he knew.

Shut up, Lilith thought, *don't ask any more questions.*

'Why was that man all bandaged?' she heard herself say.

'Because he'd had an operation.'

'Who did it?'

'The man next door.'

'Is he a doctor?'

'A surgeon.'

'And those people who visit him…'

'Patients.'

That was their game: if she asked a question, he would answer. As though he knew Lilith and her friends were so insignificant that they could even be told the truth.

She had seen him that afternoon in one of the bars in town, seated at a table and surrounded by strangers who listened to him respectfully. Lilith had been spending the last couple of hours putting up adverts for the guesthouse on all the lamp posts. She had stopped her bicycle to observe him and didn't even carry on when she saw Tomás riding on ahead without her. José was the only one talking. He was staring into the eyes of the people around him just like a snake charmer. He barely moved his hands and arms and made long pauses in which no one dared to say even a word. He said something a few minutes later that made everyone burst out laughing. He put his hat on and finished off his glass of sherry in one gulp. Immediately everyone stood up to say goodbye, even the women. Lilith saw him leave the bar with one of the men, a blonde several years younger than José.

She followed them at a safe distance, pedalling slowly.

Two blocks later she saw them go into a veterinary clinic. The gestures of respect of the blonde man were so excessive that he looked like a caricature. Even from a distance, it was evident that he could barely hide his uneasiness. Lilith leaned the bicycle against a car and walked over to the pavement. José was shaking hands with the owner of the place before following him into the back.

Overcome with curiosity she went into the clinic.

There were a couple of hamsters inside that were running like mad around a wheel. There were cages all over the place. Puppies, cats, rabbits, canaries… She stopped in front of a fish tank. The place was simple but immaculate. Voices came from the back, German voices. Lilith crept down the hall like a ghost.

Leave, she thought, but she continued forward.

She saw José through a partially open door checking the inside of a freezer that the owner of the place was showing him.

'Tonight I'll free up half,' she heard the owner say.

'I need all the space.'

The owner nodded without offering the least resistance.

'I'll need a padlock for it.'

He nodded again. Lilith had the impression that he would agree to anything. The offer the blonde man had made him the day before was too good to reject. He had offered to cover all the veterinary's fixed expenses during the time José worked with him. All he required was discretion and that he agree to all the demands made by the man who would come by the following day. True to his word, the owner began to clear the freezer on the spot, while José wrote something on a piece of paper and gave it to the blonde man.

'Do you have any friends in the local hospital?'

'Several.'

'Tell them to place this order by phone. It'll arrive as medical supplies.'

An explosion of barking suddenly erupted behind Lilith. All of the cages were barking at the same time with rage, impotence and desire, going after a Pekinese on heat passing by in the road in the arms of her mistress. Moments later the owner of the vet clinic discovered Lilith in the hallway.

'What are you doing here?'

José looked up inside the room and saw her.

'She's here to see me.'

The owner went up front. José handed his passport to the blonde man, who said something else in German before saying goodbye. Lilith didn't understand a word. She stood frozen, waiting for José to be alone before taking a few steps in his direction. José let her approach, while he took a few things from his case.

'I'm going to start to think you're following me,' he said.

'I start school today,' Lilith answered.

José put a few boxes in the freezer.

'You're going to work here?'

He nodded without looking at her.

'On the cows?'

'Among other things.'

'Then you're going to stay a long time.'

'Are you already tired of me?' he asked smiling. Playing with her was such a pleasure.

Lilith looked up and smiled. José knew children well, even their smallest movements. He knew instantly that something had happened to upset her but that he could make it right.

'I'm ready to keep my promise,' he said.

'What promise?'

'To teach you… Isn't that what you wanted?'

Lilith shrugged her shoulders, but she managed to say yes.

'We could meet…'

'Today,' his dwarf nymph said, for whom life was a matter of infinite urgency. 'After dinner.'

'I'll be waiting for you.'

'Where?'

'In my room.'

'At nine o'clock?'

'Whenever you say.'

'At nine,' Lilith said.

'Do you have any plastic dolls, in addition to Herlitzka?'

'I've got a lot.'

'Bring the doll you want to start with.'

How could she tell him she no longer had Herlitzka? That Wakolda was the one sleeping hidden between the sheets in her grandmother's bed?

Minutes later, back at school, surrounded by children singing the German national anthem, Lilith couldn't think about anything else… If there was something that she saw clearly as a twelve-year old it was that Wakolda did not have a European's hair. She had to gather up enough courage to tell him she had given Herlitzka away and they no longer had a mould. He was never going to forgive her for giving it away after he himself had saved her from deformity. The school's choir, from a small platform, was leading the singing, while the flag-bearer and her escort were raising the Argentine and German flags. Down below, the rest of the students, the professors and school authorities were also singing as if their life depended on it. The students were arranged by year and formed into rows on the strict basis of height. Lilith had won out over the next shortest by at least half a head. Resigned to being the strange one, she accepted her place in silence. She kept her eyes on the ground, hearing the laughter and whispers about how tiny her body was. She pretended to sing, although she barely knew the words. She just about gathered up the courage to watch what was going on around her halfway through the anthem. She looked her future classmates over, halting her gaze on the tallest boy in the row, who was the only one who wasn't singing either. He looked like he was as uncomfortable in his body as Lilith was in hers. He had wren-like feet and angry eyes. He didn't even look up when the director welcomed him in German.

When the programme was over the students were herded into their classrooms. Lilith saw Tomás disappear in the opposite direction and felt more alone than ever. They introduced her as the *new student* in a classroom that had barely ten students. She was afraid to ask what had happened to the rest of the students who had stood in formation with them in the courtyard.

'Your mother told me you don't speak German, but you understand it,' the teacher said, after pointing out which desk would be hers.

Lilith nodded.

'Then you'll learn fast. This is the group that speaks Spanish.'

She looked at the others before asking, 'What are we called?'

'The transition group,' they all replied in precarious German.

The teacher nodded, smiling, and added, 'As soon as you attain a basic grasp of German, you'll be transferred to the other group, which is about twice as large.'

The first day a group of blonde boys, who considered it their duty to score the girls in swimming class, shouted *Null!* in unison, which left her petrified on the tile on which she stood. Primo Capraro's covered pool had a row of steps on one end, opposite the stairs to the diving platform. Five older boys with athletic builds sat there waiting for their turn, shouting at the girls every time the teachers weren't around. Two large-breasted girls, who received a nine, shoved Lilith towards the diving board as they explained the game, cruelly savouring the details. They said that Lilith ought to feel proud because although the blonde boys had once given someone a two, they had never had a zero.

It was night-time when José returned to the guesthouse and the chimney and the lights of the house were already glowing. Through the large windows he could see Enzo sitting at his desk, with an eyeglass over one of his eyes, held in place on his forehead, painting the lips of one of his porcelain dolls. Seated next to the fire, Eva was sewing one of the blonde linen wigs with Lilith's help, who was preparing the fringe. Polo was playing with an electric train on the pinewood floor. They were the picture of happiness. He slowly walked around the house like a hungry predator. Unaware they were being observed, no one looked up. Lilith was the only one to sense a movement outside in the pine trees closest to the house. She leaned her forehead against the window, but she couldn't see anything beyond the autumn wind that was beginning to strip the leaves from the trees. She slowly walked around Enzo, watching the steady artisan's hand with which he painted the outline of the doll's lips. Eva turned the volume up on the radio and motioned for Polo to turn off the electric train. The melodramatic voices of soap opera actors were reaching the climax of a scene of betrayal. Lilith took advantage of the silence to think about the best way to tell them what she had decided to say several hours ago.

'Papa,' she said, when the programme ended.

Enzo took a few minutes to look up from the eyebrow he was finishing painting in a perfect arch.

'I want to do the treatment. Mama said I should talk to you.'

Enzo exchanged glances with Eva. They had spent the last few days discussing the matter. Eva was convinced that there was nothing to lose by trying it out. The two knew how much it hurt Lilith to see how small she still was and compare herself to how fast the other children of her age grew.

'I'm not afraid of the shots. Besides, they're not dangerous.'

'There're always risks, even when he says there aren't.'

'But it's my body…'

'You're underage.'

'What's that got to do with it?' Lilith snapped angrily.

'We decide what to do with your body.'

Enzo swapped brushes to do the tiny row of teeth. The finality with which he spoke put an end to the conversation. He set Lilith on his lap and placed the brush in her left hand.

'You do the teeth.'

He patted her as he adjusted the eyeglass on her. It was a way of telling her everything would be all right. Lilith painted the two front teeth in pearly white, but without Enzo's steady hand. There was less than half an hour until her meeting with José. At that very moment he was walking down the dim hall in the guest wing when he heard laughter in one of the rooms. He stopped when he saw Tegai reflected in the mirror. Tomás was kissing her with a young man's urgency, his hand between her legs and her dress pulled up to her waist. When she looked up, the Welsh girl saw the German in the mirror of the dresser. She pushed Tomás away and returned to making up the double bed as if nothing had happened. Tomás immediately left the room, straightening his clothes. He passed by clumsily without a word, so excited he could barely walk. José occupied himself for a few moments watching Tegai's efforts to calm her desire as she spread the sheets and buttoned her dress.

'Are you expecting someone?' he asked.

'A couple of French tourists are coming tomorrow... Are you going to eat in the dining room or should I bring you a tray?'

Without looking at her he said no and fixed his gaze on the grandfather clock in the corner. It was eight-thirty. He barely had time to take a bath before receiving her.

She took one of her oldest dolls and yanked its arms and legs off. It was her way of telling him she hadn't forgotten his promise and she couldn't wait to begin.

Five minutes before nine she hid three pillows under the sheets and patted them into the shape of her body. She opened the window and walked out into the gutter that wrapped around the house. Although it was the end of the summer, the temperature still dropped considerably at nightfall. It was especially chilly that evening, with a freezing wind coming off Nahuel Huapi. Lilith concentrated on not looking down. It was a long way to the ground. She only had one hand to balance herself. She carried in her other hand a doll she'd cut in pieces. She tried a couple of windows on the left wing until she found one that was open. It was José's bathroom. There was steam on the windows and the tiles were damp. There were footsteps on the floor that disappeared as they went off in the direction of the pinewood floor. A tap was dripping, and time seemed to stand still. Lilith stopped and took a deep breath, but even then the air was insufficient. The mixture of fear and excitement had brought on a mild asthma attack.

It wasn't the first time.

She leaned against the edge of the bath until she could feel the blood in her head again. She took a few steps along the hall and stopped again. It was wrong for her to be here at this time of night without anyone knowing where she was. She was about to turn back when José appeared in the doorway.

'You're late,' he said.

Lilith nodded, petrified.

'Come in.'

He moved aside so she could get by.

Lilith obeyed.

The smell on the inside was even stronger than in the hall. Sticky sweet. José set his suitcase on the desk and set out the tools for what they were going to do: thread, filament, needle, tweezers, scalpel. He had everything, even gauze and alcohol, as though it were a living being and not a piece of plastic.

'Did you bring her?'

Lilith placed the severed pieces of the doll on the bed. She assembled them on the desk like the jumbled pieces of a puzzle.

'Have you ever sewn anything?'

'Never.'

'Today you'll learn how to.'

He opened the desk drawer and took out the dagger with the double S and the emblem in German. Lilith pointed to a symbol she had seen before in the photographs from her mother's school.

'What's that?'

'An ancient good luck symbol… The swastika.'

He cut two pieces of filament with precision, with which he threaded two needles.

'The four branches represent the possibilities every mortal has: to achieve liberation, go to hell, be reborn as a man or be reborn as an inferior being.'

Lilith took one of the needles as she studied the emblem.

'And what does it say there?'

José read the inscription in German and then repeated it in Spanish.

'My honour is loyalty.'

'What do blood and honour have to do with each other?'

'Racial mixing makes the blood impure and destroys memory.'

'Is my blood pure?' Lilith asked.

After a few moments' silence in which he considered explaining the consequences racial mixing had had on her body, José picked up a needle and one of the arms.

'No,' he said.

He motioned to Lilith to take a leg and the torso.

'Every stitch must be an imaginary circle. It goes into the plastic like this and comes out the other side… See? Like a dance. Without stopping. One stitch and then another and then another… Now you.'

Nothing was as easy as it seemed when you saw him handling the needle like a magic wand. Lilith's needle stuck in the plastic the first time and the second time the filament became knotted and she pricked the end of her finger on the third try. She dropped the needle with a sharp cry of pain and went to put her finger in her mouth. José caught her before her tongue touched the drop of blood that glistened there like a crown on her finger, dark and perfect.

'There's nothing more mysterious than blood,' he said holding her hand as the drop increased in size. 'Paracelsus thought it was a condensation of light.'

He squeezed her wrist as if he meant to choke her. Lilith thought there was something hungry in his look, something that made her think about vampire stories. But even though it hurt, she didn't ask him to let go.

'What do you have to remember?' she asked.

'What?'

'You just said racial mixing destroys memory…'

'Yes.'

'What do you have to remember?'

'Who we were.'

'When?'

'In the beginning.'

'The beginning of what?'

'Of everything.'

He let go of her hand. Lilith raised her finger to her mouth and sucked. Her blood was warm and sweet. She held her finger against her palate a few minutes before asking:

'Who were we?'

'*Sonnenmenschen.*'

'*Sonnen…*'

'*…menschen.*'

'What's that mean?'

'The *men of sun*, the *men-gods*, the *man-wizard*.'

'A kind of *supermen*?'

José smiled.

'Something like that.'

Lilith picked up the needle again.

'I think you're a little crazy,' she said.

She dug her needle into the plastic. For the first time she managed a decent stitch. In five minutes she'd sewn up a piece of the mutilated thigh. She'd sewn the pieces so tight not even a millimetre of movement was possible. Before, they could turn completely. The stitches were too visible and they were all in different places. There was another drop of blood on her finger as though the tiny wound refused to close. José couldn't stand it. He opened the drawer, took out his black notebook and stuck his hand way in the back. He put a small leather box on the table. It held pipettes and small glass plates one inch by an inch and a half.

'May I?'

Without waiting for an answer he grabbed her hand again.

Lilith nodded. Something told her it was no use resisting. Even if she'd said no, José would have grabbed her thumb and placed it on one of the plates. He placed the drop of blood on the glass surface and let her go as he hurriedly placed another plate on top. Her blood sat trapped between them.

'What's that for?' Lilith murmured.

'It's a sample. So I can see how much more you can grow.'

She watched him in silence while he put the plate away after having marked it with an L. José opened his notebook to a page he'd marked. He made a rapid notation and then closed it.

Lilith couldn't take her eyes off the notebook.

'What are those drawings for?'

'Which ones?'

'The ones in the notebook.'

He couldn't stand the intrigue any longer. He couldn't explain how she'd seen them, because he never left the room without locking the door. And he never took the notebook from the room.

'How do you know I made some drawings there?'

Lilith paused.

'I saw them.'

'Do you have a key to this room?'

'No.'

'Then, how'd you find out?'

Lilith nodded towards the window, still looking at him. *Brave*, José thought, delighted by her guts. There'd be time enough to punish her later.

'What did you see?'

'I saw us… My family.'

Quick as a flash he came to the same conclusion Lilith had a few days earlier. If his little friend opened her mouth, he'd be out of the house the next day. Something had made her keep quiet. And there she was with him at that hour of the night. Now he understood why she'd been so upset recently.

'I like to draw people I know.'

'Why?'

'To understand them.'

'That's why you jot down their measurements, their weight…?'

'Poets write what they see, painters paint it, I weigh and measure everything that interests me.'

'Do we interest you?'

'You interest me.'

Lilith turned red. She was at the age when she could be convinced of anything.

'You interest me.'

'Why?'

'Because you're different.'

She was afraid to ask any more questions.

She hugged the plastic doll. She had to hold onto something familiar.

'Do you want me to go or stay?'

'Stay.'

'You know if you tell anyone our secret I'll have to leave…'

'I'm not going to say anything.'

She was telling the truth. At least for the time being she was going to keep her mouth shut. And he didn't need much more than that.

Moments later, Lilith returned to her room along the dark hall. Her head was so full of the guest who now lived under their roof that she could think of nothing else. No one had ever paid so much attention to her.

7

Accustomed to the jokes, whispers and laughter that her tiny existence provoked, Lilith spent her afternoons in the library. She didn't go to swimming class or P.E. again and she didn't even bother to walk around the courtyard during break. The only place she felt safe was among the silent rows of books. Every time the bell rang she hurried to hide herself in her cave. If she heard any catcalls or nicknames (albino dwarf was the favourite one) she just kept going, head down. The librarian lost no time in offering her something to do, dusting the dozens of volumes that were stacked at random. During the war years when the school had closed its doors, the books had been kept safely in the attics of a dozen illustrious inhabitants of the city. Once they were in their new quarters, the librarian faced a pharaonic task: the classification of hundreds of books, labelling them and creating a catalogue. It was the perfect ruse for Lilith to disappear from the schoolyard. In exchange, she could take some of the volumes home with her, the chaos was so great that no one would notice some had been taken. On one of those afternoons, while she was looking for the word *Sonnenmenschen* in a German-Spanish dictionary, she saw, through one of the bookcases filled with dozens of old books, the boy from her class with the angry eyes. The teacher had taken it upon herself to introduce her to each student one by one. Wren-foot's name was Otto and he didn't bother talking to anyone. He was standing in the next aisle, tearing the pages of a book into strips, which he then tore into smaller and smaller pieces, which he then put in his trouser pocket. He tore up a book in a matter of seconds and grabbed another. Lilith watched him, intrigued. She had seen him on more than one occasion striding rapidly through the halls. Every so often she caught him looking at her, but Otto never tried to talk to her. She drew a little closer so she could see what book he was tearing to pieces. The movement made Otto look up. Lilith turned to look at the dictionary, pretending to be lost in concentration, but a moment later Otto walked over from his row to see what book she had in her hands.

'What are you looking up?' he asked when he saw it was a dictionary.

'Sonnen…mens…'

'*Sonnenmenschen*. You won't find it there.'

He turned around at the end of the row when he saw Lilith was not following him.

'Follow me,' he ordered.

Otto walked over to a corner of the library. He seemed to know it by heart. He stopped at the last row, the only one Lilith had not yet visited. It took him a full minute before he found a hardcover book covered in dust, *The Race of the Future*, by Edward Lytton. He turned some pages until he found a chapter titled *Sonnenmenschen: the sun-men*. An illustration showed a man taller than normal, something like an Aryan Adonis. Standing behind Lilith, almost three heads taller but light years away from Aryan purity, Otto smiled with a cynical smirk.

'Did they really exist?' Lilith whispered.

'It's a bunch of hooey.'

'Who says it's hooey?'

Lilith turned to look at his trouser pockets.

'Why do you do that?' she asked.

'Do you know what's going on in the world?'

'What is going on?'

Otto hadn't been able to think about anything else for days except his new classmate. She was the strangest person he had ever seen. He knew what she said was true. She didn't have the faintest idea of what was going on.

'Are your parents German?'

'My grandparents were,' Lilith said.

Without saying a thing, Otto handed her *The Race of the Future*.

'Read it before I get to it.'

He shoved the book scraps down in his pockets, leaning down a foot and a half to look her in the eye.

'And you'd better keep your trap shut.'

That night, hidden under the sheets, Lilith read the book Otto gave her from beginning to end, a short novel that described in unusual detail an origin of Nordic men who reached the Andean high plains as representatives of a special race. *The Door of the Sun of Tiahuanaco* and *The Return of the Wizards* were so cryptic she couldn't even begin to understand them. Much less the books by Helena Blavatsky, Guido von List, Rudolf von Sebottendorf and Churchward. But she would never forget those names because the librarian had asked her to pull them out from the others so she could put them on one of the highest shelves. Lilith sensed immediately that it was the area of forbidden books. That arrangement was her reading guide. Everything they took out of circulation passed through her hands. In order to understand them, she first expropriated the German-Spanish dictionary that served as her compass during the long nights she spent submerged under the sheets. Her dedication was so extreme that in less than a month she grasped the general meaning of a sentence, although subtleties escaped her. In her second secret visit to

José's room she carried the dictionary in her pocket and set herself to translating a couple of headings of a genealogical tree on the first page of the black notebook. An organisation complete with arrows and numbers. The first word she looked up, underlined more heavily than any other, was *Endlösung* (final solution). The next ones were *Aussiedlung* (evacuation) and *Sonderbehandlung* (special treatment). There was a list on the second page full of numbers and names that branched out under the heading *Vernichtung durch Arbeit* (extermination via forced labour). The third page had the header *Ahnenerbe Forschung und Lehrgemeinschaft*, which Lilith managed to translate as *Society for the Study of Ancestral Heritage*. The heading struck her as so strange that she put the notebook back, certain her translation was wrong. She scrambled out of the window only minutes before the Chevrolet could be seen coming up the dirt road that led to the house. She knew the German's habits by heart. He intrigued her so much that she hardly slept at night, speculating about his origins and where he would go next.

José wasn't sure why the possibility of making toys made him so excited. He had got into his head the idea of making a perfect mould and, like so many other obsessions, it barely let him sleep. After all, it was an inoffensive pastime, a way of experimenting on achieving perfect forms. He had never been able to wait without doing something, and that was all he could do now, wait. The day before he had spent a long time walking between rows of toys. All their stuff was second-rate. During his walk he stopped by the office of the Justice of the Peace, where a friend worked who had offered to help him with anything he needed. But José's request, somewhere to make plastic molds, could not have seemed to him more unusual.

'May I ask what for?'

'Dolls.'

The man nodded, convinced that the real reason lay behind his expressed interest, contraband of some kind, like money, jewels, documents…

'Give me a few days,' he said.

José exited without another word. As he drove back to the place that he had begun to consider his home, he came to the conclusion that the time had come to move forward. Two months after opening the guesthouse on Nahuel Huapi, the family had become used to living with guests in the house. No one was quieter than the German. Some nights the guests ate together and he was the only one to sit at a separate table.

He had achieved his goal, which was to go unnoticed.

He parked the Chevrolet beside three cars of strangers and walked over to Enzo's workshop, which in reality was a small room at the back of the garage. He could see him through the windows, pouring some liquid porcelain into a metal mould with a space for head, body, arms and legs. Tomás was next to him, polishing a recently fired porcelain head with a nylon stocking, making its skin smooth. He knocked and walked around looking at the design for fingers and moveable necks that hung from the walls.

'I didn't know you were interested in this,' he said.

He was lying. It wasn't the first time he had watched him work. He had spied on him a dozen times and seeing him mould the porcelain bodies was what made him conceive the idea that those dolls should be perfected and mass produced. But only now did he have a concrete proposal to make to him.

'It's just a hobby.'

'It's more than a hobby. There's talent here…'

The workshop was Enzo's private world. Pliers and paintbrushes lay on the workbench like scalpels. Paints, pots of porcelain, loose arms and legs, some piled up heads… He opened the door of a brick oven he had built with his son's help. There was barely room for two moulds. He put some asbestos gloves on before removing the mould in the oven.

'Careful, it's molten.'

Tomás made room for him. Enzo set the mold on the workbench and carefully opened it. Inside was the head, the body, the legs and the arms of a doll, perfectly fired. Enzo smiled with childlike enthusiasm. He set about, under José's watchful eye, assembling the members, using liquid porcelain to join them.

'You would have made a good surgeon, Enzo.'

José also smiled and for once his enthusiasm was not feigned.

'How many do you make a week?'

'Only a few, two or three.'

'And how much do you sell them for?'

Enzo couldn't help blushing. It embarrassed him even to think about giving them a price. Beyond the amount of time it took him, he understood clearly that the dolls were the work of an amateur because of his makeshift resources.

'Who'd I sell them to? I give them away…'

'You shouldn't.'

Tomás looked up from the body he was polishing, surprised at the vehemence of the comment.

'They're works of art, not trinkets. If you sold them like you should they'd fetch quite a bit… There are no dolls like these in Bariloche.'

He pointed to one of the many illustrations tacked to the walls: moveable glass eyes, held in place by an iron frame inside the doll's head.

'What's this?'

'Harebrained ideas I'm never going to do anything with,' Enzo said.

José smelled resignation behind the offhand comment. Lilith's father was much more talented than he thought and not only with porcelain. He was skillful in all the manual arts. His specialty was mechanical things and motors were his passion. He spent hours inventing objects that he didn't have the courage to show to anyone. José waited for him to put the recently assembled body in the kiln for a final firing.

'Have you ever thought of mass producing them? You could make dozens of dolls exactly the same and turn your dreams into reality…'

'That costs a lot,' Enzo said.

José smiled with the calm of a bullfighter preparing to give the final thrust.

'Not if you find an investor.'

'Who would want to…?'

'I would,' he interrupted him.

Tomás exchanged glances with his father, both equally surprised. José picked up his case and his hat.

'I'm proposing a good deal to you, Enzo. Think about it.'

He exited the workshop without another word. There would still be time to convince him, if necessary. Although judging by the glow in Enzo's eyes when he heard the offer, it might be enough for him to take the bait on his own. In the best of moods, José whistled as he walked the half-dozen yards that separated the workshop from the guesthouse. He turned down a couple of invitations to dine with other guests and sat down at his own separate table. Luned came in with a mushroom risotto and a show of enthusiasm for that day's main dish.

'Are you sure you don't want to try the lamb? It's very tender meat and will melt in your mouth…'

She was the sort of Welshwoman without any charm, timid and plump, her hands always damp. He said no without even looking at her and, fifteen minutes later, he sat down to drink a herbal tea on the veranda that looked out over the countryside. He heard Lilith's laughter before he could see her emerged from the dark, chasing some fireflies. She persevered until she got one. She was still somewhere between being a little girl and a woman. José watched her, rocking in an iron chair that squeaked with each movement. He had her come over to his side and leaned over to look at the bug caught in Lilith's cupped hands.

'It's a female,' he said.

'How do you know?'

'Because of the size… Do you know why they glow?'

Lilith said no without taking her eyes off her prey.

'It's to attract the males in flight. If they feel threatened, they deactivate the glow. Open your hands a little…'

Lilith opened her hands a half inch. Without asking her if it was all right, José stuck his index finger into the dark little cave that served as a prison for the firefly. He pressed it against Lilith's left palm. She tolerated the tickling sensation, a combination of disgust and pleasure, stoically. In an instant, the firefly stopped glowing.

'See?'

'How do they do that?' Lilith murmured.

'Bioluminescence. Underneath each cuticle there's a special organ that emits light.'

'Are you making this up?'

'Why would I make it up?'

'It's impossible to know everything.'

Lilith had closed her two palms together with his finger still caught between them.

'What happens when the male comes along?'

'They copulate. The female places the fertilised eggs underground. The larvae come to life four weeks later. They're called glow-worms… They feed on snails and slugs. They paralyse them with a liquid that digests the body of the mollusc and then they suck up the nourishment.'

'That's yucky.'

'Not very different from what you did?'

'I drank milk.'

'And the worms puréed slug…'

Lilith laughed, delighted to be flirting with the realm of the scatological.

'They feed in their lairs until they turn into nymphs.'

'What's that?'

'It's the highlight of their lives. It barely lasts twenty days.'

He withdrew his finger. The firefly took advantage to escape through the same opening. It disappeared into the dark before Lilith could catch it.

'And then?' she asked

'It turns into an adult, copulates and dies.'

Lilith stood looking at the dark space between her cupped hands and then looked up at him. She couldn't resist the temptation to ask him.

'How much more can I grow?'

José smiled. He had no idea it would be so easy.

'With a little help… quite a bit.'

A month after installing himself in his new routine, José received a call to say that the growth hormones had arrived. José knew the intelligent thing was to stop all his activities, but he preferred to accept the measure of risk involved rather than sitting and waiting for his capture for the following months. He already had several potential clients: calves, cows, pregnant women with anaemia problems… Even Lilith's parents had agreed to a two-month trial.

They told their daughter the evening before she was to begin treatment.

'I'm going to do the treatment too,' Eva said.

'So you'll grow?'

'To improve your brother's growth.'

'Sister,' Lilith said.

'Whichever.'

When he had seen that Eva felt measurably better thanks to the iron and vitamins he had prescribed, José suggested that a minimal dose of growth hormones would be beneficial for strength during the final months of pregnancy. He showed her books, photographs, statistics and bombarded her with a flowering rhetoric, not letting up until she said yes. Enzo held out for days until his own doctor confirmed to him that the German's proposal was hardly crazy. On the contrary, he suggested she could not be in better hands. Enzo came away from the consultation more paranoid than ever. His doctor was German and a friend from Eva's childhood. More than once he had seen him chatting in the bars in town with José, who had much more of a social life than he did. But Eva had made up her mind and he didn't have the heart to go against her. The pregnancy had made her irritable and tired. The first afternoon, he had the two of them come to his study, where he prepared the two syringes in front of them. He took a vial from the box of dry ice in which he transported it and rubbed it with his hands until it attained room temperature.

'What's that for?' Lilith asked.

'It hurts more if it's cold.'

As he filled the syringe, José felt surprise at the fact that he was worrying about someone else's pain.

'Who's first?'

'I am,' Eva said.

She let him clean her arm with a ball of cotton dipped in alcohol and let him jab her without protest.

'Done.'

Eva applied pressure to the cotton ball. She trusted him. She'd felt better the past two weeks thanks to the vitamins. She had begun to grow fond of the German, who couldn't be kinder to her children. More than once he had offered to pick them up from school, which was four blocks from the vet clinic. The two boys fought for his attention.

It was different in Lilith's case.

The first erotic charge left her fascinated and she melted whenever the German looked at her body. She let him undo one of the buttons on her dress under the watchful eye of her mother.

'I have to give it to her in her belly.'

He pinched her flesh with the tip of his index finger and his thumb and wiped it with the damp cotton.

'You're going to feel a prick, like a sting…'

Before finishing the sentence he had already inserted the needle.

'Did it hurt?'

'Not at all.'

'I told you it wouldn't.'

He made her stand next to the doorframe and put a ruler on her head. He asked Eva for permission to make a mark that would allow them to keep track of her growth. He measured Lilith's height, barely four feet.

'This is how tall you are today,' he said as he pointed to the small mark on the cedar. 'We'll see how tall you are in a month.'

'What if I don't grow at all?'

'It's all a matter of faith,' José said.

Some weeks later, one of the cows, to which he'd started giving high doses of hormones halfway through her pregnancy, gave birth to perfectly healthy twin calves. The rumour spread throughout the countryside and a number of people opened their doors to the German veterinarian. What nobody mentioned was that, in addition to vaccinating their cattle, some of them agreed to sell blood samples of their children and pregnant wives for a few Deutschmarks. José had returned to gathering statistics and couldn't conceal his good mood.

PART TWO
WAKOLDA

8

Feeling more drunk than in love, she didn't feel quite well again until she plunged her head underwater in the lake the next day. It was the last warm days of autumn and the leaves had already turned. After plunging in the freezing waters of Nahuel Huapi, Lilith bobbed up and down until she felt her muscles going numb. She danced like a siren (the bottom half of her body was perfect). The fifth time she broke the surface she saw José sitting on the dock, watching her. He had brought a small chair and umbrella down to the beach. She came running towards him along the beach, her bathing suit clinging to a body that began to take on the curves that would leave the little girl behind. She was a small bundle of body tone. Her teeth were chattering and her nipples were hard. Lilith saw the desire in his face and arched her body as much as she could as though wanting to show off for him. It was the first time the look of a man made her feel that way.

'Would you like to come in with me?'

'I don't like the water,' José said.

'Have you met the new guests?'

'I just did.'

'What are they like?'

'They're French,' was all he replied.

They had arrived that morning, a pair of sharp noses travelling on a year-long trip through Patagonia with a video camera. José paled when he saw them in the dining room area of the common room that morning, recently bathed with their skin tanned by sun and wind. The man cleaned a camera lens while the woman had her hands in a black canvas bag. She explained it was a sort of homemade darkroom where she developed the film they had shot, taking the film off the spool and placing it in a tin container. Their plan was to document all of South America before heading home. They already had more than thirty tin containers they mailed to a post office box in Buenos Aires.

'It's a good time to be a long way from Europe,' the man said.

They had arrived from Ushuaia. They had travelled for six months to the far south of Chile and crossed over from there to Argentina. They had two still cameras. Besides the landscape, they took pictures of the people they met along the way.

'So, if you'd allow us…'

'I don't like photographs,' José interrupted.

That was all he needed. Two imbeciles laden with cameras and good intentions. He said no more than was necessary and found the first opportunity to flee to the dock. The Frenchman did not insist. He also knew that these were not times to be asking questions, but he was a professional agitator and the German accent had irritated him from the start. Enzo ordered a kid goat that day to celebrate his youngest son's birthday. They cooked it over a slow fire with a dressing from Extremadura that filled the house with its aroma. He couldn't accept the German's vegetarianism and thought it almost an illness or a bad vice that could be corrected with a few plates of meat. In any case, the Frenchman monopolised the conversation with an abundance of anecdotes, allowing him to surreptitiously spit out his chewed piece of goat, which he threw underneath the table. The English mastiff devoured it immediately and licked the pinewood floor clean. José could barely stand the nasal accent of the Frenchman,

122

his unrestrained laughter, the false humility with which he told how he had scaled volcanoes, mountains and glaciers, travelled up the Amazon, lived in leper colonies, escaped an avalanche in the salt mines outside Cuzco, rescued a dozen workers from the collapse of some gold mines in Bolivia... Overwhelmed by so much phony heroism, he was on the verge of escaping to the bathroom when a new turn in the conversation made him stay where he was.

'Veritable concentration camps,' he heard the Frenchman say. 'They had ten-foot high barbed wire, with hundreds of Mapuches starving to death without anything to eat...'

'I don't know anything about it,' Enzo said, looking at Eva with alarm. 'Have you heard anything about it?'

'Never.'

'What year are we talking about?'

'1879. My wife's grandfather was Welsh. He wrote about all this in his memoirs. We came here to film the ruins of those camps... After the campaign and the defeat of the Indians the frontier policy swung into action. Every time they found an indigenous family, they would deport it to some other territory... I've heard of between ten thousand and twenty thousand Indians who went through those concentration camps. They even had to open two special cemeteries in '79, which gives you an idea of the magnitude of what happened. The other policy was to prevent births among the group. They separated the women from the men, the children from their parents and changed their names... Many know they have indigenous roots but they can't reconstruct their family history because their forefathers were called Juan Pérez. The truth is that the ruling class of time divided up the spoils... Even the newspaper *El Nacional* ran from time to time the headline: "Indian distribution today"... Upper-class women would go to the Immigrants Hotel on Wednesdays and Fridays to look for children to give away and maids, cooks and all sorts of servants to exploit. They broke families up without a second's thought.'

'How horrible,' Eva murmured.

She didn't stop to think about the fact that a lot of the young native women and peons who had worked in this very house when she was a child were the descendants of those children who had been torn from their parents decades before. Lilith looked at her parents to see if what the Frenchman was telling was the truth. She saw her father cross himself silently. José was the only one who had a strange smirk on his face, a mixture of a smile and uncertainty. He couldn't believe what he was hearing. In the end, they hadn't invented a thing.

'The war was fought with the pretext of protecting the pioneers on the frontier, but they never got any of the handouts. Neither the former frontier inhabitants nor the Indians that remained… What they did was create a vast empty space for the large landowners, ranchers from Buenos Aires or London. After twenty-seven years the state had given away for pennies almost five billion square miles to landowners and their patrician families.'

When they got up from the table, all except José weighed a few pounds more and it was not just because of the kid they had eaten. The Frenchman had a talent for casting blame on his listeners, something he did with true devotion. When he offered to take their picture in front of the house, Eva and Enzo felt a little ashamed to be there, standing smiling in front of a mansion they had inherited through no merit of their own. They gathered their children around them and made them stand up straight. It was an important occasion, their first family photo. The Frenchman promised to develop it that same night in the darkroom he had set up in the bathroom.

When he saw the lens pointing toward him, José lowered his chin, hiding his face under the brim of his hat, and turned on his heels and retreated toward his car in a rage. The well-intentioned imbecile had made him a fugitive in his own house. If there was anything he couldn't tolerate it was him showing everyone those photos goodness knows where, precisely at a time when the bloodhounds had torn away his anonymity. He floored the accelerator, turned to look out of the rear window and sped off down the path that led to the entrance to the road. He had to think of something. It would be the last time he was the one to take flight. When he turned to look ahead he saw Lilith running toward the car. He opened the passenger door and she jumped in.

'Let's go.'

'What are you doing?'

'I'm going with you,' she said, still agitated.

'Did you get permission?'

'I don't need to.'

'Lilith…'

She turned toward him and smiled.

'I'm not going to harm you, so don't be afraid… Let's go.'

José gave in.

Once they were on the dirt road, Lilith put the radio on and turned the dial back and forth until she found a Charlie Parker number. José looked at her out of the corner of his eye. He hated this music of trumpets and saxophones, but said nothing. He watched her undo her two braids with her eyes shut, before opening the window and sticking her head out. Her hair, long, blonde and loose, went wild with the wind. She could feel him looking her over. She felt light and pretty.

'Do you like jazz?' José asked.

'What's that?'

'You were humming…'

'Oh, I didn't know.'

She looked at the lake stretching out in front of them.

'Do you know that Lake Gutiérrez used to be called "The Eye of God" in the Tehuelche language? And in Tierra del Fuego there was a lake called "Horizon's End". Now its name is Monsignor Fagnano. He was the priest who carried the cross with the troops.'

'Who told you that?' José asked, although he had an idea.

'The Frenchman.'

He was going to have to do something about that man. Urgently. Before he rotted the head of his little pupil.

'Where're we going?'

'To see a monument.'

'In town?'

'No, a little further out.'

He turned onto the main avenue in the direction of the Hotel Llao-Llao. They had given him exact instructions: you go fifteen miles until you come to Villa Tacul. It was one of the first questions he asked the colleagues who received him, if the bunker was still there. It had been built a decade before on the banks of Nahuel Huapi, seventeen miles east of Bariloche. This allowed easy access by water for large boats. At that time, the hide out in Patagonia was a dot on the map for him in a far corner of the world and not a real geography like the one he now inhabited. They told him it was really there, although only the rubble of what it had once been. Two years previously, seventy elements of the Argentine army had dynamited it during the night. The explosion was heard in town, a low boom that shook the beds where the inhabitants of Bariloche slept. The next morning a thick black cloud could be seen in the distance. In only a couple of hours they had done away with one of the secret refuges of the retreating empire.

If you plan on visiting it, you'd better not wait much longer, they told him.

It was rumoured that they were going to clear the remains. The order had come down from above that they wanted to do away with any trace of it.

'How much further?' Lilith asked.

'We're almost there.'

He turned to the right at Villa Tacul without going into town and advanced a little more than half a mile until he came to the edge of the lake. They were in the middle of nowhere. Restless, Lilith stayed behind in the car. Her fits of courage were brief. But this time her prank had taken her too far to go running into her mother's arms. José got out of the car and walked to the shore. The forest was thick. It was incredible to imagine that they had got through it with machinery, men and cement to build the refuge. When he turned around he saw Lilith standing next to the car, wide-eyed.

'We go on foot from here,' he said.

He walked toward the forest, certain that she would follow him like an obedient puppy follows its master, even if he smells danger. He moved a branch aside to let her by.

'Do you want to go first?'

'No, I'll follow.'

A nearby noise made her grab his arm. The trees had closed over their heads. The light was fainter down below. José was wearing long trousers, but Lilith only had on a dress that came down to her knees… After a couple of yards she was covered in scratches from the branches and thorns.

'Come up here,' José said.

He pointed to a piece of trunk covered with moss and turned to offer her his back. Lilith only hesitated a moment. They were too far away for her to say she wanted to go back.

And something about the adventure, being there like that, alone, amused her. She climbed on his back, putting her hands on his shoulders. José held her by placing his thumbs under her thighs. He'd never had her that close or her legs spread so wide for him. But he had to hold in check any temptation that might weaken her trust.

'Are we lost?' Lilith asked.

'No, we're just fine. Don't be afraid.'

He could feel her breath on his neck. He rested his two thumbs in the hollow where her thighs ended, a piece of her skin no man had ever touched before.

'A poet said once that love is an act that cannot be realised without an accomplice.'

Lilith, who had no idea of what cynicism was, asked, 'Who's the accomplice?'

'You are.'

He advanced a few yards more in the direction they had indicated to him. It took him a few minutes to find it, so thick was the vegetation that had already covered the remains of the bunker. He set Lilith down on one of the chunks of stone.

'Here we are.'

If he had brought her here this far it was because he had always hated to be alone. He needed a court of buffoons, although in his present state of poverty it meant only a little girl. He was wracked with nostalgia, standing there, in the rubble of his dreams, alone and with no future. He took a few steps, looking for something more than the few pieces of stones that remained intact...

There was nothing.

Watching him walk around, Lilith divined that something was not right. His gestures began to show impotence and rage.

'I'm cold.'

He didn't answer, having forgotten her completely. He walked towards the shore and leaned against one of the larger stones that was still intact. He muttered something very low under his breath, as if to maintain an imaginary conversation with someone who wasn't there. Lilith realised when she drew close that he was murmuring scattered words in German that sounded like insults.

'Are you all right?'

Lilith didn't dare touch him, so immense was the distance she suddenly felt between them. She waited in silence, standing next to him, until it began to drizzle.

'I want to go, José.'

'We'll leave when I say so.'

It wasn't the way he said it. It was the look he gave her, barely an instant's glance. In a blink he was no longer the refined and aristocratic gentleman who delighted her. It was that someone else, the most sadistic assassin ever, who made her turn around and flee toward the forest without thinking about the direction she took.

All she wanted to do was to get away from him.

It was no use. She only got a few yards before she felt his hand on her left arm. He stopped her by force and picked her up, kicking with rage. He begged her pardon. He shouldn't have treated her that way. Lilith made an effort not to cry in front of him, but she couldn't contain herself. He looked at her, helpless and tender, standing on the remains of the Empire with her palms turned toward him.

'Lilith,' he said, savouring the sound.

He suddenly realised that he'd had women, but he'd never had his *Lilith*. He had always been fascinated by that other woman spoken of in the unabridged Genesis, the one in addition to Eve.

'Do you know what your name means?'

To his surprise, she nodded and opened her mouth to say without hesitation, 'A friend told me there exists a legend among his people about an evil woman called Lilith who kills all children born of the female.'

She was crying harder than ever and he could barely understand her. José smiled.

'Is there any other way for them to be born?'

'I told him the same thing, that all children come from the female and that the female is woman and all children are born of woman…'

'And what was his answer?'

'He said I was Evil and refused to talk to me again.'

It wasn't the only bullying she'd received in Primo Capraro. Everyone in the group who spoke Spanish at home was under the watchful eye of *The Germans*… That was what some of the ones who spoke German called themselves.

'If I tell you a secret, will you stop crying?'

Lilith nodded.

'Thousands of years ago, men were Gods. A race fallen from the stars. Lucifer was one of those gods. His name meant the Most Beautiful Light… *Luci-Bel*. He had entered through the Morning star, Venus. Lilith was the wife of that first man… His faithful and eternal lover.'

José failed to tell her that she helped him give life to his own immortality by killing her children. And that he was convinced that Adam's true name was Lucifer.

'Isn't Lucifer the devil?'

'That's a Christian lie.'

He dried her tears with his hands. One of the storms had passed, but the other was about to break over their heads.

'And what's this?'

'A temple.'

'*Blitzkrieg*,' Lilith said.

'What?'

'Just a few minutes ago, down by the lake, you were repeating that, *blitzkrieg*... What does it mean?'

'What comes after the thunder...,' he said, searching for the word.

'Lightning.'

'That's right. Lightning. Lightning war.'

He moved away without another word and walked around the ruins in silence. He was looking for a door, but couldn't find it. There was no longer an inside, as he had dreamed. The ruins of the bunker were nothing but some scattered stones.

'*Blitzkrieg*,' he heard Lilith repeating behind him.

They would only have been able to win that way, with a short hurricane-like war. He had asked himself a thousand times what would have happened if the Führer had invaded England, if he had taken the king prisoner and reinstalled his brother to the throne... Because that's where the tragedy of World War II began, with the belief that those were sacred territories, the last remains of the disappeared polar continent. Invading them meant the eventual collapse of the Empire. Germany without England would not be able to sustain the stability of a New World... Lilith kept her distance, watching his physical and mental wanderings without daring to tell him her bones ached with the cold. She asked for nothing, not even when it suddenly started raining over their heads. It was the first time she had seen him like that, desperate. Although she had no idea of what those ruins meant, she could tell their importance by the devastating effect the state of the bunker had on José.

They were silent on the way back.

Lilith knew she was going to be punished for disappearing like that for several hours and without telling anyone. But she couldn't think about that. Everything she'd done up to that point seemed like child's play.

'We'll say you ran into me on the road,' she said a few yards from the house, watching the storm out the window.

José nodded in silence, concentrating on the road he could barely see beyond the windshield. Nothing interested him less than her and her drama. Years later Lilith would still remember that trip as the moment when she understood José was fleeing from something or someone.

It was a case of flu rather than any punishment that kept her locked in her room for days. Her fever reached 104 degrees. She ached in all her bones and muscles and even her scalp and eyebrows hurt. Nevertheless, she didn't tell her mother that José had doubled the amount of hormones. He had done it the first time Eva allowed her to go to the German's room alone, harried by the large number of guests that had showed up for the long weekend. Lilith saw him use a whole vial to fill the syringe rather than only half.

'That's more than before,' she said.

José nodded in agreement, flicking the syringe with his middle finger and thumb. He wasn't surprised to see Lilith noticing the difference. Every afternoon she paid full attention to his work.

'I'm giving you a little more from today onwards,' José answered. 'So you'll grow more rapidly…'

Under Lilith's hopeful gaze, he rested his index finger on the mark and raised it almost two inches.

'When you reach this point we'll be able to demonstrate that it's working.'

Lilith promised not to say a word to her parents.

She began to become obsessed with her height. She no longer knew if she was worn out from the fever, the chemicals or the effort she was putting into making her body grow. Even then, the scratch on the cedar door frame took two weeks to increase by only a few fractions of an inch. More than once she woke up in the middle of the night and went from one end of the house to the other, barefoot and without turning any lights on, to stand against the frame of José's closed door. A recurring nightmare took her back to the first movie she had seen in the town's only movie house.

'It's a horror movie,' Otto had promised her when he invited her.

Lilith didn't have the courage to confess to him that she was totally ignorant of film genres. She just asked him what that was, her gaze fixed on the poster next to the ticket booth announcing the movie. *Teenage Zombies* she read, written in blood red letters. A young blonde was screaming as she stared into the camera, imprisoned in a cage.

'You're going to have a hard time sleeping tonight,' Otto concluded, smiling as they settled into their seats.

Minutes later the entire movie audience screamed while on the screen two young women, who had been kidnapped on an island by a mad woman scientist and an army of zombies, were imprisoned in a glass capsule and gassed to brainwash them. Lilith joined in the screaming, euphoric over so much shared fear, and she even grabbed Otto's arm when she saw one of the zombies throw himself on top of the star.

'Do you believe in zombies?' she asked him on the way out.

'No,' Otto replied, although he didn't sound convinced.

'I do.'

The fear imprinted itself on her unconscious. Lilith always awoke from her nightmare just as she was about to join the army of zombies. One such night when she opened her eyes choked by a muffled scream, she heard the music, laughter and voices that came from the neighbouring yard. She clutched Wakolda and opened the window. Everything indicated that a party was in progress on the other side of the hedge. She tried to make something out, but the vegetation was too thick. She began to be obsessed with finding out what went on in that house... Who were those men and women who came and went by hydroplane? Why did they never go out during their stay? Who was the owner of the house? The neighbour's black car had come for José at the hotel more than once. The chauffeur waited for him with the door open. Lilith knew the car. She had seen it coming and going from the neighbouring mansion and she had seen it in the streets of Bariloche... A movement caused her to look down. Seated on the frame of the window, she saw José come out of the door on the left wing, dressed as spiffily as ever. Surprisingly, instead of walking toward the Chevrolet, he crossed down through the yard in the direction of the lake. Without wasting a moment, Lilith pulled on some rubber boots and ran down the stairs. Seconds later she saw the outline of the Gersman strolling calmly among her grandmother's rosebushes. He seemed to know exactly where he was going. When he came to the last ledge that dipped down into Nahuel Huapi, he veered to the right and was swallowed up by a stand of pine trees and acacias that was so dense that no one ever walked there.

Lilith stopped at the edge of the forest.

While she was telling herself to retreat, her feet moved forward.

She followed José's footprints along a path that was so narrow that there was barely enough room for an adult to pass. She had only been there a few times in her life, when she played hide-and-seek with her brother. Seconds later she heard a door open a couple of feet away in another curve of the path.

She stood without moving.

José greeted someone in German.

The door closed with a squeaking sound. The voices of dozens of people in the distance were singing the Nazi hymn *Horst Wessel Lied*. Lilith knew it by heart. It was the favourite song of a number of kids at school. A live band of musicians joined the voices. Lilith moved forward a little bit more until she stood in front of the neighbour's hedge and the iron gate that joined the two houses. She could barely move, camouflaged by the clinging vine along the wall.

9

The German employee at the Justice of the Peace's office didn't give up until he found the factory for the plastic moulds. He found it in Trelew, hundreds of miles away from Bariloche. He travelled there personally to make sure that the machines were capable of making dolls before informing José that he had kept his promise. An exhaustive survey of the wealthy families of the city had put in the hands of the most admired scientist of the Third Reich the only imported doll to be found in the vicinity of Nahuel Huapi. José had known for a long time he needed to find another doll as delicate as Herlitzka to use as the basis for his new moulds. He confirmed it the night he asked Lilith to lend him her doll.

'What do you want it for?' she asked, not looking him in the eye.

'To use it as a mould… We're going to convince your father to make perfect dolls. And in large numbers.'

The next afternoon she dressed Wakolda in a French-cut dress, Herlitzka's favourite. She fixed her hair in braids that she carefully wound around her head in a typical Tyrolean hairdo her grandmother had taught her. She placed the native clothes she wore when Yanka gave her to her in a box and wrapped Wakolda, who was still the same doll even though she was now disguised as European, in a small lace blanket. In José's room, she took the injection without batting an eye and waited for José to write down the daily dose in his black notebook before parting the folds of the blanket to show him what was hidden inside it. José looked at the wood and plastic monster. He smiled, as if it were a joke.

'What is this?'

'Wakolda.'

'And Herlitzka?'

'She's back on the road in the desert.'

'Did you forget her?'

'It was more like a… swap.'

'You exchanged Herlitzka for *this*?'

'Yes.'

'May I ask why?'

'I don't know.'

José removed the European disguise. His hobby had been destroyed before it began. He was not going to find in Bariloche another doll as perfect as Herlitzka. He studied the features of the Mapuche doll. Her arms and legs were made from paradise wood, but her body was cloth. Bits and pieces of cloth that weren't even enough for that. Her belly was as swollen as that of the pregnant girl in the desert. Her features had been carved by hand and were a mass of imperfections. Seeing the disdain with which he looked at the doll, Lilith covered Wakolda with the blanket. José had spent the past months reading about the dangers of racial mixing in the Argentine territories. Before being decimated the aborigines had made up a third of the country's inhabitants. Sarmiento and Alberdi were already convinced that European blood would improve the quality of a population consisting mainly of Indians and Creoles. Wakolda was the proof that it wasn't worth wasting time on the monsters of such a mixture.

'She's useless for the mould… But we can play with her for a while.'

'Play what?'

'At transforming her.'

'No, not her.'

She left the room without letting him touch her. José called the employee at the Justice of the Peace's office the next day. In addition to the factory we would need to find an imported doll that could serve as a mould.

He had almost forgotten his little hobby when the employee called round to visit him at the vet clinic where he worked a few half days a week. He brought with him the imported doll and its clone, dressed down to the last detail like her twin sister. The employee had had his sister-in-law make two identical dresses and the best wigmaker in the city formed a blonde wig made with his daughter's best curls. José's smile, as he examined the clone front and back, confirmed to him that the undertaking had been a success. The employee would remember that handshake the rest of his life and with greater emotion than the birth of his children.

'Let me make it clear that this will be quite expensive…'

'The money is not important,' José interrupted him.

He placed the two dolls on the back seat of his car and stood looking at them… They were far from being what he wanted, but the challenge made him feel the vitality that he thought he'd lost. He was going to exchange the linen hair for real human hair that he would affix with wax by hand and with a needle. He wanted real eyelashes, movable glass eyes, fingers and necks that could bend and clothes made by hand. He started the car, captivated by the possibility of soon having dozens of identical babies, perfect in their dimensions, with blonde tufts and turquoise eyes.

If only flesh and blood ones were as easy… he thought.

Emotion kept him from completing the sentence.

While he waited for Lilith and Tomás to come out from school, he discovered with surprise that the doll was the synthesis of all his research, the perfection of the immortalised species. Days before, standing on the ruins of the bunker, he had understood more than ever the importance of giving signs to his people that they were biding their time there, hibernating... And for this they needed symbols that would embody their hope. When Lilith climbed into the back seat, her brother was already inspecting the imported doll and its clone lying on the back seat.

'Which would you say is the original?'

'This one,' Tomás said.

Filled with joy, José told him he was wrong. On the way home he could talk of nothing else but his plans in which he hoped to involve Enzo. It was getting dark when he pulled up in front of the neighbour's locked gate, hidden in the vegetation. He honked his horn a couple of times before a man came toward him. He recognised him and opened the gate without asking any questions. Lilith exchanged looks with her brother when they saw the car pulling forward along a road bordered by trees.

'What are we doing here?' she asked.

'I have to give a friend a present.'

The car went about seventy-five yards before stopping in front of the house.

'Take them out,' he ordered Tomás.

A woman dressed in what looked like a combination of a nurse's uniform and a housedress received them. She smiled when she saw Lilith, looking her up and down. José asked them to wait outside and disappeared with her into the inner labyrinth of which Lilith was only able to see the first 200 feet, replete with closed doors. Ten minutes later, when he came out, he no longer had the clone of the imported doll. But he brought with him good news. The owner of the house had bought a TV and he had had the idea of buying one for them. It was only a matter of time before the channels from the capital could be seen in Bariloche.

'You can't live cut off from the world,' he said with his usual impunity. 'It's important to know what's going on outside.'

Back at the guesthouse, he went to find Enzo to tell him the news. Now, instead of him being just an investor he had a concrete proposal to make to him. Getting straight to the point, he proposed the job to him and asked his permission to hire the most robust of Luned's cousins, a Welshwoman of laconic sentences who spent the day in a corner of the kitchen mending clothes and sheets on a sewing machine. José had noticed some time ago her simple tastes and how she combined bits and pieces of fabric as if she had been trained in a Swiss girls' school. When José explained to him that he needed someone who could give form to his ideas, Enzo plucked up the courage to show him the flexible little arm he had been working on, with ball bearings in the base of each finger. Tired of spending his days on the upkeep of the guesthouse, the proposal excited him from the start. José told him he was planning to rent a small place and he would like to put it in his name. Enzo didn't ask why he preferred not to be named in the contract. Although he sensed something out of the ordinary, life was a lot easier if you pretended not to notice.

He accepted.

It was the first time in his adult life he had made an important decision without consulting his wife. The deal he made with José cost him more than one argument with Eva, who could barely stand the complicity between her husband and the German. Now he ate with them every evening. They were so excited by the project that they continued to make plans while they ate. Crazy with enthusiasm at having found a mentor willing to finance his dreams, Enzo had invented in only a few days a mechanism of gears to move the hands and he designed metal hooks to attach the arms and legs to the body and even came up with some options for José's wildest idea. He wanted the dolls to have a smell. He wanted them to smell like almond oil when hugged by their owners. Two weeks later, Eva, who lived with her feet more firmly on the ground, began to get irritable. She demanded a timetable from Enzo. She wanted to know when they would order the dolls, how much they planned on selling them for and how much profit they'd make. José, on the other hand, was only concerned about how long he could stay in Bariloche. It had been years now since life in exile had stirred him as much. But his colleagues were beginning to get restless, always wanting to know how much longer he planned on staying.

'A few weeks,' he'd repeat.

It was an open secret that Mossad had ordered agents to stop looking for him, for fear that a simultaneous operation would endanger the arrest of Adolf Eichmann, who had had a greater responsibility in the apparatus of the Nazi state. After him they would undertake the second operation. José had a half dozen informants reporting to him on almost a daily basis about any news that would precipitate his escape. He had already studied all the routes across nearby borders. Several colleagues of the utmost trust would collaborate with his escape when the moment came.

But he wasn't going to allow anyone to rush him.

None of the options seemed to him as attractive as his current abode. The night when a half dozen armed men arrested Eichmann in an outlying neighbourhood of Buenos Aires, José was eating an Estremadura stew with his adopted family while he decided how many plastic arms, legs, torsos and heads to order from the factory in Trelew. The very moment they were throwing Eichmann on the floor of a rented car, he raised his glass in toast.

'Here's to a business deal that you can keep in your family.'

And he added after a dramatic pause, 'Even when I'm no longer with you.'

'Cheers,' Enzo shouted, his chest filled with emotion.

'May I ask you something?' Eva interrupted, the only one with dry eyes. 'Why are you doing this?'

José smiled at her with the calmness of a bullfighter who readies the final thrust.

'To multiply, madam... It's the key to success.'

'How does a couple of dolls multiply anything?'

'The taste for beauty. If I can make good and lovely things... Why not show others how to make them?'

Lilith couldn't help sighing.

She had a knot in her throat when she clinked her glass against that of the man who had hypnotised her. She was as enchanted as could be and the thought of a future without him seemed intolerable. Eva, on the other hand, excused herself and got up. Sometimes she felt as if Enzo was a stranger she barely knew. She lay down on her parents' old bed, but not even there did she feel safe. The complicity she sensed in each round of laughter between her family and the German guest irritated her. Her youngest child was running around the sitting room among the chairs playing disconnected notes on a recorder. José followed him with his eyes, more alert than a shark. At eight o'clock sharp he offered to help Enzo put them to bed while the latter finished doing the calculations of the number of dolls with which it would be prudent to begin operations. Without waiting for an answer, he picked the youngest up in his arms. A handful of the imported sweets he carried in his pocket kept him quiet when he tried to protest. There was nothing easier to win over than the heart of a child.

'You, too,' he ordered Lilith and Tomás, 'off to bed.'

They got up immediately, thrilled by a night that broke with routine. Enzo smiled when he saw him exit with his flock, more obedient than ever. On the way to their bedroom, the youngest dodged a few attempts by Tomás to grab the recorder from his mouth and played a few deformed notes as loud as he could.

'Quieten down,' José said.

And the enchantment worked a second time because they obeyed. For a few steps in the dimly lighted hallway, surrounded by children, he was reminded of his better years. He knew without a doubt he would never again live anything remotely similar. In the boys' room, he ordered them to get into their pyjamas. Tomás already had hair under his arms. He undressed the youngest. It had been a long time since he'd had such a fragile body in his hands and he drew out the moment, mindless of how the child was shivering with cold when he pulled the nightshirt over him and put some flannel socks on his feet.

'Read to me,' the youngest commanded.

He pointed to a bookcase full of books. The vagueness of his gesture confirmed to José that he could choose any book. He ran his eyes along them until he found the one he wanted. There was a drawing on the first page of a man playing a flute for dozens of children. He read:

'Thousands of years ago the city of Hamelin was infected with rats. One fine day a flute player appeared who offered his services to the inhabitants of the town. In exchange for a fee, he would free them from the plague. The villagers accepted

143

and he began to play. The rats came out of their holes and began to run to where the music was coming from. The flute player walked toward the outskirts of town and they all followed him, dancing to his music. He went toward the river and the rats, which were following him, drowned in the water. His mission accomplished, the man went back to claim his fee, but the villagers refused to pay him. Furious, the rat-hunter sought revenge. While the townspeople were at church, he began again to play his strange music...'

José looked up. They were asleep. Nevertheless, he read the final sentences. He hated leaving things undone:

'Then it was the children who followed him to the sound of the music and leaving the village behind, he took them to a cave. They were never seen again.'

The hand of the youngest was lying in abandon on José's leg. He studied the white lines on his fingernails. A lack of calcium. His thumb was misshapen from years of pressing it against his palate when he sucked it...

What was he going to do in Paraguay or in Brazil? he wondered.

Cuba and Ecuador were out of the question. He hated tropical climates. Beaches, sand and the sea, the landscape where he was going to die, all annoyed him. More than anything he detested poverty, which eliminated half a dozen Third-World countries. Attacks of panic assailed him at times when he felt the calmest.

He made an effort to think about something else.

If he had known that Eichmann had been arrested, he would have halted the project with the dolls. But the capture was kept shrouded in tightest secrecy for another five days until he had been sent to Israel. By that time, after paying an initial visit to acquaint himself with the factory and to be certain that the owner had understood the design and the list of materials, they received the call they were waiting for. Their order was ready.

They got an early start, planning to reach Trelew late in the afternoon. Enzo drove, so enthusiastic over the adventure that he told José stories about every volcano, river, lake and national park along the way. Lilith sat in the back-seat, having begged to be allowed to miss school. The plan was to drive straight through, but a few miles from Esquel, going through a national park near the Chilean border, they stopped the car. José had heard stories about the largest and oldest trees in the world, the *Fitzroya Cupressoides*, known as Patagonia cypresses. But nothing could have prepared him for their size. Even when she stood in front of the smallest ones, Lilith looked like an ant. Twelve people holding hands were needed to encircle the largest ones. A few were more than 3,000 years old.

These are not trees, José thought, *they're monuments.*

His psychotic sensibility was moved by the purity of the species. He rested his palms on one of the oldest of the trunks and closed his eyes, overwhelmed. Enzo had to beg him to get back in the car if they wanted to make it by sunset. They did not stop again until the town of Los Mártires, where they bought petrol and stretched their legs. José drove now because Enzo had started to get drowsy near Paso de Indias, the same place where the Argentine army had massacred hundreds of Tehuelche Indians decades before. They had left behind them some time ago the tropical forests of the area of El Bolsón and the road into Trelew was once again the same uninhabited flatlands of the road through the desert.

Drugged by the unbroken landscape, Lilith slept the last six hours of the trip, stretched out on the back-seat. More than once, José caught himself looking in the rearview mirror at the unconscious body of his small friend and asking himself if it wouldn't be a bad idea to take her with him, like someone stealing a pet so as not to feel lonely. When the telephones in the guesthouse began to ring back in Bariloche to alert him to the news being carried in all the newspapers in Argentina, José was already hundreds of miles away, betting on the number of heads the factory had waiting for them.

Fifty sets of arms and legs, fifty heads and fifty torsos greeted them when they entered the main room of the factory that specialized in second-rate Argentine toys. José's investment and the contract that stipulated each of the materials to be used in making the dolls enabled him to purchase an imported porcelain that had never before been used on any other toy. The result was apparent a mile away. The skin looked smooth and healthy, the colours glowed and the forms could be moulded with a previously unimaginable subtlety of detail in the folds of the skin, the nails, the earlobes, the lips, baby wrinkles and nipples. Thanks to Enzo's designs, the fingers of the hands, the knees and the elbows could bend and had the mobility of a flesh and blood baby. The result was a realism that was so overpowering that the limbs scattered over a long table constituted an unsettling spectacle.

Lilith stopped to observe the twenty-odd women who manually polished each one of the porcelain bodies. The heads were the final detail on an assembly line in which handicraft prevailed over the machines. Using asbestos gloves and long metal tweezers, two men were in charge of removing each one from the mould and hanging them from some wooden clips aligned symmetrically in five parallel rows. She walked along in front of each eyeless head trying to spot any difference. They were still warm and had none of the imperfections of the dolls her father made. Through the heads she could see a couple of employees who were sewing by machine small identical outfits: tiny angel-like dresses made in the exact same colour as the uniforms of the Third Reich. In a dark corner of the room, two employees were ironing the little wigs that others were inserting by hand into a small nylon cap. The small finished wigs, all dyed blonde according to instruction, were piled in a wicker basket. José's smile convinced them they had managed to impress the investor. Given the amount of money he had been willing to invest to achieve his goal, they could not allow him to leave the factory dissatisfied. As a present, the factory owner handed José a wooden box with a hundred tiny glass turquoise buttons.

'What are these?' Lilith asked.

'Eyes,' José said.

He put a button in the palm of her hand. It had the outline of a pupil. A hundred tiny bubbles were encapsulated in glass. Their colour was perfect, one that he had spent years seeking unsuccessfully. The owner motioned to one of the women employees to hand him one of the heads. He lined up in one corner of the table the six pieces that would constitute each body.

'Would you like to assemble the first one?' he offered.

As if it were a ceremony, José removed his jacket, rolled up his shirt sleeves and put on the glasses he carried in a leather case. They all stood around him in silence. He began with the arms and legs, leaving the head for last. Each piece snapped into the trunk effortlessly. One of José's demands had been that the dolls could be taken apart by their owners. The applause was crowned by two bottles of the best Patagonian honey liqueur which the owner kept for special occasions.

'They will be ready first thing tomorrow morning,' he promised.

'I'll take them unassembled.'

'Excuse me?'

'It's always easier to transport the pieces.'

'As you wish. All that's left are the details.'

He pointed to ten employees situated in the best place in the room, under the only window that bathed in light the table where they were working. They all had a magnifying glass fastened over their right eye by a metal band. With utmost concentration, they were painting the outlines of the lips, eyebrows and eyelashes.

'Would you like some personal mark?'

'Such as?'

'Moles, birthmarks, blushes, scars, eye shadowing, gums with teeth, tattoos…'

'Nothing,' José interrupted him.

'Well, now is the time…'

'I want them unblemished.'

An employee at the head of the line held one of the glass buttons with a pair of tweezers, about to affix it into its place. It was Enzo's proudest invention, what made it different from any other doll. The inside of the head carried the two metal clips that would hold the eyes. A tiny lever would extend out from the neck of each doll, camouflaged by the golden curls, which would allow the eyes to move. José hovered over the women, crowded by the factory owner who fluttered around him like a fly.

He leaned over the woman with the tweezers.

'May I?'

The woman nodded without saying a word. She immediately stood up and stepped back. José gave his place to Enzo.

'It's all yours.'

'You mean it?'

'Of course.'

Enzo sat down in front of the doll. All that was needed to finish her was to insert the eyes, seal the head with the second half of the cranium and apply the wig. He positioned the eyes in the socket and tightened the pliers on the inside of the head. An employee helped him to fasten the other half of the head with liquid porcelain. Holding her by the neck, Enzo moved the eyes from one side to the other until the doll looked at him for the first time.

'Perfect,' José murmured.

Rarely in his life had something satisfied him so fully on the first attempt. Success usually came after dozens of frustrated attempts, when his eardrums were already ringing with his children's screams of pain. By contrast, this had been so easy...

10

José took it upon himself to make reservations for two rooms in a resort on the outskirts of Trelew. As they had agreed by phone with the employee from the Justice of the Peace, there was a lit torch at the gate to light their way. There were seven rooms for guests in the main ranch house, which had seen better days. The walls were covered on the outside by ivy and climbing plants. There were stuffed heads on the inside: stags, hares and wild boars that were the owner's trophies, an Austrian who had come to Argentina in the twenties. Although José had expressly requested his identity to be kept in strictest confidence, the fanaticism of his colleagues was his worst enemy. Just to be able to say they were in contact with him made them capable of anything, including putting his life at risk. They had a meal waiting for him when they arrived, set with the tableware they reserved for special occasions. The Austrian's two daughters had been dressed as if it were a wedding. The family's welcoming smile was nothing more than the confirmation that the rumour was true: it was he.

'Welcome,' the Austrian said in appalling German.

The reply, curt and in Spanish, indicated to the man that he had to keep in check his admiration until José made some sign to him. He helped them unload the bags with the plastic members and he refrained from any question when he saw the dozens of arms and legs that filled the bag he got to carry.

'Through here,' he said, indicating the way.

The rooms were at the end of a passageway with walls of clinging vines. Lilith extended her hand, the tips of her fingers caressing the leaves which were still damp from the evening dew. She could barely contain her excitement. It was the first time in her life she was to sleep in a hotel, without her mother and her brothers. The Austrian stopped in front of two adjacent doors.

'These are your rooms... Who's sleeping in number 3?'

'We are, Lilith,' Enzo said.

The room was not any different from the ones in her grandmother's house, with wallpaper and floral sheets, wooden furniture and stone floors. But so much adrenaline was coursing through Lilith's blood that night that everything felt special.

'May I choose which bed?' she asked.

'Sure.'

Enzo set the bag with the plastic heads in front of the wardrobe while Lilith plopped on her back on top of one of the mattresses. The Austrian set the bag with arms and legs next to the heads. He couldn't understand why José was carrying around bags with pieces of dolls in them in the middle of the night. The fact that he was accompanied by that man and little girl had to be meant as a distraction, since they were looking for a man on his own. Why else would he need such heavy baggage?

'Dinner will be served in fifteen minutes, Mr...'

He was about to say *Mengele*, but caught himself. He could barely believe he was about to serve dinner to Nazism's most brilliant scientist. That simple anecdote would serve as bait for dozens of admiring tourists.

HE SLEPT HERE

He was going to engrave that on one of the headboards the next day. He stood standing in the passageway, listening in the shadows without daring even to breathe. He was even surprised by an erection when he heard the water running in the shower.

Lilith turned the tap on a few minutes later.

As she was undressing, she heard José singing an Italian opera. She covered her mouth to keep from laughing. He howled, struggling to reach the notes intended for a tenor.

Ma il mio mistero è chiuso in me,
Il nome mio nessun sarpà! no, no
Sulla tua bocca lo dirò!

His voice broke on the last note, but he forged ahead.

Quando la luce splenderà,
Ed il mio bacio scioglierà il silenzio
Che ti fa mia!...

Lilith couldn't contain herself. She planted both feet on the pipes and pulled herself up, holding onto the edge of an exhaust fan that connected the two bathrooms. She could see José through some grime-covered slats, his arms extended as though he were on stage addressing an audience. His mouth was open, his eyes were closed, the edges of his nostrils tense, his head turned slightly toward the ceiling... His nakedness, seen from above, was comical, with his bald spot and his prominent belly. There was no mystery, no elegance, no authority. Everything was on view, damp and pudgy. Lilith had found what all of the German's enemies had sought: the perfect image to destroy years invested in the meticulous construction of an image. She ducked her head when she sensed he was about to open his eyes. She jumped down, her arms and legs extended, with all the calmness of a ninja who knows where to land even when jumping backward. Enzo banged on the door when her feet touched the damp tiles.

'Hurry up, Lilith!'

'I'll be right out!'

She was enchanted beyond all hope. Far from frightening her, what she'd seen added to the adrenaline, which kept her electrified. It was only because of the period of drowsiness that she was able to stand so much intensity, with equal portions of excitement and tenderness. Excitement because she had never seen a naked man. And, no matter how unimpressive the image, you never forget the first time. Tenderness because of the very audacity and surrender she had seen in someone who pretended so hard to be in control of himself. Ten minutes later, when they met up in the hotel's dining room, she couldn't contain the attack of laughter that welled up from her throat like an erupting volcano to burst forth right there in front of everyone.

'What's the matter, Lilith?'

She tried to say something, but all you could hear was a tiny voice drowned out by spasms of laughter.

'So... rry...'

'What are you laughing about?'

'Noth... ing...'

'That's enough,' Enzo ordered.

'I'm happy... Is that bad?'

She couldn't help it. Everything made her laugh, José's seriousness, his clothed body, the curtness with which he asked for a bottle of wine, Patagonian lamb and a green salad.

'Weren't you a vegetarian?' the owner asked, only to snap his mouth shut, realizing he had said too much.

Enzo looked up startled from the menu.

'Do you know each other?' Enzo said, looking from one to the other.

'No.'

'He told me on the phone.'

'I sometimes eat meat.'

'This is liver pâté,' the owner's wife saved the day.

They had spent the day preparing a vegetarian stew. His wife and daughters set out to harvest the most unusual vegetables in Trelew so that he would savour the taste of his stay. José spread a piece of homemade bread with the pâté and lifted it to his mouth, already transformed into a carnivore nothing repulsed. He let the Austrian serve him a glass of wine…

'It's on the house…'

…begging him to stop being so obliging. But it was no use. The daughters spied on him from the half-opened door of the kitchen and the man's wife only had to look at him to blush. He was certain they would be telling the whole world about it tomorrow, just as various colleagues in Bariloche must have done. He cursed his bad luck. Thanks to these traitors he couldn't postpone his escape any longer.

Maybe you'll learn your lesson, he thought. He wasn't going to be so trusting in the next place. After all, it was his own fault. No one had forced him to contact the network in the south.

Enzo had already seen the deference with which several strangers had treated him during the trip. There was no doubt in his mind that his guest was much more famous than he admitted. He swore he would not share his suspicions with Eva. He wasn't about to run the risk of possibly missing out on the business with the dolls. It had been years since he'd felt so alive. He felt surprised at himself momentarily for the lack of scruples behind his thoughts. The moment he allowed himself to think that way was the definitive death of the young romantic idealist he had been. Lilith, who happened to be watching him, suddenly understood her father had grown old. His shoulders were clenched around his neck. She put a hand on his. Enzo swallowed a piece of bread he had spread with a large chunk of pâté and dropped the knife he was using to devour everything in sight.

'Am I eating too fast?' he asked shamefaced.

'Thank you for letting me come.'

'Oh, well… Sure.'

'Eat more slowly. It's not good for you.'

'Yes, yes, I'm sorry…,' Enzo said and dropped the bread.

They smiled at each other, intimidated by the tenderness they felt looking at each other. José took it all in, deeply perplexed. It was not the first time the unconditional love between parents and their children had upset him. He had never been able to feel anything even remotely similar toward his parents or his offspring. It was not a lack of sensitivity, because he cried like a baby at his favourite operas. He arranged a couple rosemary sprigs before taking his first bite of Patagonian lamb. He liked to define himself as a defender of beauty.

The differentiated focalisation of emotion, he thought.

Enzo was dozing off even before the meal was over. In addition to driving hundreds of miles, he had been exhausted by the effort to maintain an intelligent and articulate conversation with his German guest, who seemed to know everything. About to fall asleep in his chair, he asked to be excused. Lilith begged him to allow her to stay up a little bit longer. She had slept half the way.

'I'll keep an eye on her,' José said.

He suggested they drink a cup of digestive tea on the veranda facing the countryside. Lilith rested the bottoms of her feet on the edge of the steps with her heels sticking out, rocking back and forth slowly while José studied the first doll he had assembled in the factory. He was whistling softly, taking his time going over his creation.

'They're going to take it from our hands,' he said after a while.

'Who?'

'Our friends.'

Lilith looked at him with surprise. She didn't know they now shared friends. The Austrian came up behind them, carrying a tray. He knew he was interrupting when he was still several yards away, but his desire finally to speak to José was too strong.

'Lemon verbena tea and Patagonian Welsh cake,' he said.

'*Danke*,' José replied.

The two syllables in German functioned like a password.

'I'm truly sorry about the arrest,' the Austrian said in German.

To his surprise, José frowned.

'What arrest?'

'Eichmann's.'

José went pale and the Austrian understood he was breaking the news to him. And being the protagonist in a piece of history, no matter how small, filled him with a sense of the heroic.

'When did that happen?'

'A week ago, but they just announced it yesterday.'

'Where is he?'

'In Israel.'

José lifted the cup of tea to his lips with a steady hand. He did the maths quickly: the Mossad bloodhounds were probably just getting back to Buenos Aires, setting in motion the operation that would lead them to him in a matter of weeks.

The time to leave had come quicker than he expected. Lilith followed the dialogue in German, attempting to understand what they were saying. It was still hard for her to understand the language when they spoke like that, effortlessly and without pausing. When José told her it was time to go to bed, she followed him down the poorly lit passageway, always staying a few paces behind.

This is a goodbye, she thought without understanding why.

As if he heard her, José opened the door to his room and looked at her from the doorway. He said he was going to give her her injection in his room so as not to awaken Enzo. He seemed to be deciding how far to go that evening. He knew Lilith would have said yes no matter what. She trusted him, as so many other women before. He let her pass and shut the door.

The next morning they were on their way. Enzo felt a silence inside the car that was so thick he opened the window to allow the whistling of the wind to move the air currents that barely let him breathe. Fifty miles outside Bariloche, his German partner announced the time had come for him to leave.

'Now?'

'By week's end.'

'And the dolls?'

'I'll leave them in your hands.'

Enzo grabbed the wheel with a pang of regret. The landscape in which they were saying their goodbyes was as arid as the one in which they had met months before, although the temperature was around freezing. He looked at Lilith through the rearview mirror. His daughter had her forehead pressed against the window and there were tears in her eyes. She was chewing her fingernails as she always did when she was choked with anger. Her dress was on backward. Her arms were wrapped around the first doll the German had assembled at the factory. Enzo had just now remembered that the evening before he saw the silhouette of someone undressing in the dark. He did not recognise his daughter or the room they shared. For a moment everything looked strange and foreign.

'Lilith?'

'Go to sleep.'

'What time is it?'

'It's late.'

She was upset and he could make out she was hugging her knees.

'Are you all right?'

'Go to sleep.'

Even her voice sounded like someone else's.

Enzo at that moment felt like he was the child and she was the adult. He obeyed and shut his eyes. An uneasiness he could not put his finger on made him remember how terrified Eva was the first night Lilith went on a school camping trip. She had spent the entire night awake, possessed by a panic attack thinking about all the things that could happen to her: a car accident, an accident in the lake, the three nights they were going to sleep in the open in tents that gave them no protection at all, when they would go climbing, when they would run the Río Chubut rapids in a boat... The second day, stressed out from holding on to her from a distance, she said she had decided to hand her over to the world. *It's the only thing a mother can do to keep from going crazy*, she said.

Lilith must have known José's decision since last night. That's why he had found her still awake at five a.m., when he opened his eyes. He was convinced that that was why she was so upset.

'Do you have to leave right away?' he asked.

'Something has come up. My wife needs me.'

'Will you be going back to Buenos Aires?'

'Only for a short time.'

'Then perhaps you'll come back…'

'Maybe, yes.'

Enzo knew he was lying. They would never see him again. The same certainty produced in Lilith a mixture of relief and anger. No one asked about the nature of the urgency, knowing intuitively that he would not tell them the truth. They spent their time making plans for the future of their business. The first step was to assemble the dolls and present them to the public. Several of José's colleagues had already ordered one from him, even those who had no little girl at home. It was going to be a secret trophy for many of them, the proof that they had had contact with him. Just like the legends of the passage of Billy the Kid and Butch Cassidy through Patagonia, and many swear that their grandfathers had traded saddles with them in exchange for horses, refuge and food. José imagined, not without a certain satisfaction, the stories that would circulate for years to come about his passage through the south. One of his greatest consolations would be that, the construction of a myth. Those fifty perfect blonde dolls with blue eyes would speak for themselves. He'd decided to leave an autographed one for the first Mossad bloodhound to reach Bariloche. His plan was to prepare his escape that same night after he got back to the guesthouse. He was going to call a colleague and have him decide which car could take him across the nearest border. His belongings all fitted in the suitcase he'd arrived with. The only thing he had to do was to collect the samples he kept at the vet clinic. Perhaps the moment had come to give up even his study samples, but he had no intention of doing it. They could take everything away except his experiments.

Paraguay, he thought with scant enthusiasm.

His Patagonian cycle was ending, to be replaced by an exodus in the direction of the tropics. Nothing brought more irritation than ending up in poor and humid countries. That's why he decided he had to get it over with quickly, without sentimentalism.

Tomorrow, he repeated.

But life continued to set traps in his path.

Chaos set in that same evening.

11

Tomás came out to greet them as soon as he saw the Chevrolet coming up the tree-lined road with its high beams on. He waited beside the car, upset, his eyes were glassy with excitement and fear. Eva had begun to have contractions eleven hours ago. The midwife never showed up, whether because of the storm or because of the flu and pneumonia epidemic that had rendered one out of every three inhabitants bedridden. Lilith's tight cough and feverish state convinced José that her body was already incubating the illness. The youngest child had already fallen ill so that the only ones keeping Eva company when they entered the room were the Welshwomen. Bathed in cold sweat, Eva was moaning on the bed.

'We can't do this without a midwife,' Luned murmured, who had brought into the world six children and twenty-three nieces and nephews.

A scream coming from Eva made Enzo back away without even touching her.

'Go look for her. I'll take care of her,' José said.

Calmly, he removed his hat, coat and glasses and rolled up his shirt sleeves. Eva would have liked to ask him to leave, but the contractions were getting stronger and stronger and she was exhausted. She let him spread her legs so he could feel her. For decades the German had brought dozens of newborns into the world, and had made as many depart it. The threshold from life to death and vice versa was a place he knew by heart. All he had to do was stand in front of a woman giving birth to know if her child was going to have a natural birth or a Caesarian. This time there was no doubt. He asked Tegai for a pan of boiling water, towels and alcohol. He gave Lilith the key to his room.

'Bring me my doctor's bag,' he ordered her. 'And the dagger, sterilised.'

For once Lilith had no mind for appearances. They were running out of time. She opened the window and climbed out on the gutter, revealing to everyone her shortcut. Moments later she jumped into José's room. She was feverish. She could barely breathe because of the congestion, but she didn't stop until she found the dagger with the secret emblem, which moments later she placed on the ring of the kitchen stove where she moved the knife back and forth in the fire. She felt a stab of nausea when she thought this knife was going to sink into her mother's body. She had no choice but to trust him.

When she returned to the room, José was moistening Eva's lower abdomen with alcohol. Everyone obeyed wordlessly, transformed by desperateness into soldiers. José asked Tomás to tie his mother's hands to the bed with two strips of sheet. He didn't have enough anaesthesia to put her out and he had to keep her from flailing with her arms when the pain became too much. Transformed into an Amazon, Eva placed her wrists against the bars of the bed to make his task easier. At the end of her strength, all she wanted was for it to end as quickly as possible. José placed his hand on her abdomen. The skin was stretched so tight that it looked like it was going to split open. He studied the exact place for the knife. He rested the point of the knife and turned it a fraction, anticipating the pleasure of a perfect cut. He had always defended Caesarians. He liked nothing more than to bring out the newborns with perfect features, without the deformities and wrinkles caused by passage through the birth canal. Just like this one came out, a baby girl identical to Lilith, but with perfect dimensions. It was born with the umbilical cord wrapped twice around its neck. It took ten seconds to open its eyes and cry out. It couldn't have weighed more than four and a half pounds. Its skin was wrinkled and covered with down and so transparent you could see the veins. The palms of its hands, the heels and the feet were red. José placed the baby in its sister's arms to press the mother's womb until the placenta emerged. Lilith found herself suddenly face-to-face with the tiny body bathed in blood, barely struggling, angry at having been brought into the world too soon.

Another contraction confirmed his suspicion and he plunged his left hand into Eva's womb to extract the second baby girl. She was smaller than her sister, barely a tadpole. Her crown was enormous and was without hair, eyebrows or eyelashes. Her head was too large in relation to her body and her extremities were poorly developed. Her fingernails were soft and didn't reach the tips of her fingers. She had all the symptoms of premature birth. The bones of her head had not yet ossified, especially the occipital and parietal bones.

Three and a half pounds, he thought, holding her by her feet.

By contrast to her twin sister, the second baby did not cry.

José set it on the bed to observe it. Her breathing was rapid, shallow and irregular. It was evident that her pulmonary alveoli had not completed their development and the muscles necessary for breathing were too weak. Neither of their nervous systems had attained required maturity and her movements were slow, her primitive reflexes were almost non-existent and the same was true for her muscle tone. Tegai held her in her arms while José cut the umbilical cord to separate it from her mother. Stunned into silence, Lilith helped the Welshwomen bathe the two newborns in a basin of warm water, while José finished sewing up Eva, who did not remove her eyes from them, too weak to give any orders.

When Enzo arrived with the midwife, it was all over. Wrapped in the same blanket, the twins looked so fragile he was afraid to touch them.

'Why is she breathing like that?' he asked, looking at the smallest one.

'They need oxygen,' José said, as he took a pen from his inside pocket to write himself a note in German. 'Her lungs are not fully formed and her immune system is not yet completely developed. Her breathing problems could get worse if she catches pneumonia or has any other complication. It would be best if your children kept their distance.'

Lilith covered her mouth with another fit of coughing. José immediately motioned for her to move away. He signed the note and gave it to Enzo.

'Go to the house next door. Give this to the person who answers the door.'

He looked at Lilith, who was leaning against the door.

'Go with him. They know you.'

Seeing Enzo hesitate, he insisted, saying, 'I'll stay with her.'

Eva nodded from the bed, her face begging him to obey. Enzo looked at the room, which looked more like a crime scene than a birthing room. Everyone was covered in blood. He felt Lilith's hand in his own, but he only came to when he felt the snowflakes on his face as they waited for someone to open the gate to the neighbouring house. He looked at Lilith, who was coughing next to him, shivering in the cold. He took his overcoat off to put around her when his daughter refused to wait in the car.

'How do they know you?' he asked.

In between fits of coughing, Lilith told him about the afternoon when José went to deliver as a present the first doll to come out of the factory. Enzo nodded. She didn't have to say much more. They waited in silence while the nurse who received them the last time read José's note. The woman looked up to examine Lilith's blood-splattered dress. A gesture was enough for the man standing a few yards away to open the entry gate.

The interior of the house was not much different from the guesthouse. It had been built in the same year by architects with the same background. Enzo managed to see two other women dressed the same way. The house looked like a hotel, although a man who crossed their path a few feet away carrying serum and the wheelchair from which another man was watching the snow in the winter garden made him think of a small private clinic. The nurse stopped in front of one of the rooms. She unlocked it with a key and went in, leaving the door partway open.

'What is this place?' Lilith whispered.

'I don't know,' Enzo replied, more uneasy by the minute.

The doors of the living room were wide open a few yards in front of them. Enzo took a few steps and saw a dozen men and a couple of women sitting around a radio. They were sitting there in silence, listening to the news report. *He was transported to a safe house, where they tied him to a bed and questioned him until he confessed he was neither Ricardo Klement nor Otto Henninger*, the announcer was saying, *until he gave his real SS number and admitted that he was Adolf Eichmann*. Enzo felt Lilith's hand in his, telling him wordlessly to stop. *They made him sign a letter in which he affirmed that he was going to Israel of his own accord*. One of the women was weeping silently. But Lilith didn't look at her, nor did she pay attention to the announcer. She had just seen the clone of the imported doll, which had been placed on a marble stand between two large Persian vases and some other art objects. *A week later they put him on an El Al plane dressed as a flight mechanic. He was given a first-class seat and a false passport, on his way immediately out of the country to Haifa.* A man got up to fill his glass with whisky and, seeing Enzo, he closed the door. The voice of the announcer could still be heard from inside. *The Argentine chancellery entered a protest of the serious violation of sovereignty, taking its complaint to the UN Security Council.*

'I'm going to need your help,' the nurse said, behind him.

She was standing in the doorway of the room she had gone into moments before and she had an oxygen tank in her hand. Enzo followed her without asking any questions. Incredibly, inside was an operating room. He helped her gather up catheters, gauze, syringes and a couple of vials as she read José's note, as if following orders. The nurse helped him load everything into the car and got in without saying a word. When Enzo asked her what she was doing, she showed him José's note.

'It says for me to go with you.'

Even though the two houses weren't more than a quarter of a mile apart, the return was slow and complicated because the snow had started to block the roads. They had to abandon the car some distance from the guesthouse and carry the tanks by foot, crossing over the snow. They found José busy between Eva's open legs, sewing her up. It was a disturbing and exceedingly strange image of intimacy that Enzo would never forget.

'You've done this before,' Eva murmured to him in German.

The pain and her state of exhaustion had carried her back to her first language.

'Hundreds of times,' José replied, taking the last stitch.

'Then tell me if they're going to live…'

'They've first got to make it through the night.'

The Welshwomen helped Eva lower her legs and they put a blanket over her body. José forgot her the minute he saw the nurse come in with the oxygen tanks. He had only a few minutes to stabilise the twins. Standing near the door, Lilith listened to them talk in lowered voices. Although she worked with utmost professionalism, the nurse couldn't be less interested in her sisters. She wasn't there because of them.

'They asked me to tell you the plane to take you away is ready.'

'Not yet.'

'They said they're back in Buenos Aires. You're next.'

Without understanding a word of what they were saying, Enzo watched them place damp cloths on Eva's forehead. Working on her own, the nurse inserted a catheter into each one of the twins.

'What was it like?' José asked her.

'They kidnapped him.'

'I can't believe no one knew a thing.'

'They contacted people in Buenos Aires,' the woman said. 'No one knew.'

The twins were so weak that they didn't even cry when their skin was pricked. José immediately gave instructions for them to be injected with an array of medicines he'd ordered.

'It's not safe for you to stay here. You can find twins anywhere.'

José smiled calmly, as he listened to the body of the littler one.

'I can take care of myself,' he said, putting an end to the conversation.

The nurse nodded.

'I'll be downstairs if you need me.'

Enzo followed her with his gaze. He couldn't help but feel relieved to know that she was going to spend the night with them.

'Who are they?' he asked when they were alone.

'Friends.'

'Why are they helping us?'

José looked up from the crib, smiling in spite of everything.

'They're not helping you. They're helping me.'

Alone in her room, Lilith slowly undressed, removing each item of bloodstained clothing as though performing a ritual. He had been injecting her with growth hormones for months. Some nights the pain was so intense that she would have liked to rid herself of everything, her arms, legs, the unbearable stab of pain in her backbone, neck, forehead, arms and elbows. Even her scalp and eyelashes ached and light, cold, heat all hurt her. One minute she was shivering and the next minute she was bathed in sweat. There was an unbearable cramp in her jaw and her eyebrows bunched and her eyes watered. Her body was a battleground. José's chemicals were tentacles that travelled through her blood to her extremities, seeping into her bones and making her grow. Nobody could imagine the violence of pushing a body to grow when that was not its nature.

José was the only one who had seen suffering like this in other specimens.

But nothing at the moment could be less important. The combination of exhaustion and euphoria kept him awake for hours. He devoted himself to drawing the twins in his notebook, surrounding the twins with comments: undeveloped immunological system, weak pulmonary alveoli, primitive reflexes and non-existent muscle tone. He spent the following hours writing up the physical differences between the sisters and making calculations about their growth possibilities. More than once he had to refrain from going to the room where the twins were, more alarmed by the silence than the outbursts of crying, a howling that was joined by the cries of the child who had until that night been the youngest, angry because Tomás wouldn't let him go near his parent's room during the night.

Morning brought to José the crying of the weaker of the premature babies. There was hope if she had survived the first twelve hours. He knew he had to get out of there immediately. But he couldn't resist the temptation to postpone his trip for a few days when Eva came to beg him to accompany her to the bedroom where the twins were sleeping. The younger one was weaker than the previous day. She wouldn't feed and had spent the last hours in a state of drowsiness close to unconsciousness. *If she were a shark, her sister would have eaten her in the womb*, he thought when he saw her, tiny, pale and wrinkled like an old woman.

'Why won't she eat?' Eva asked.

'She has no sucking or swallowing reflexes. Her stomach is very tiny and she doesn't have adequate secretions to produce digestion. Her digestive system is not totally prepared to take on its functions.'

José called the nurse in to help Eva fill a syringe with mother's milk. They placed her against the headboard of the bed and attached the syringe with milk above her shoulder, with the tube that went directly to the older of the premature babies. With infinite patience, José helped the twin to latch onto Eva's breast, even though the nourishment came from the tube connected to the syringe. He explained to her that the baby would figure out that the food was coming from the breast and he calibrated the quantity of milk in the syringe:

169

four centimetres every three hours. It was absolutely necessary she get nourishment to complete the growth process.

'Please stay a little longer.'

Two days, José swore to himself.

He couldn't care less for the suffering of his adopted family. But he felt a strange adrenaline in extending his Patagonian stay to the utmost extent advisable... And he was fascinated as always by the great mystery of his life: twinning effects. It only took a couple of phone calls for a car to arrive at the house before noon. Enzo helped him take the incubators out from the car and take them up to the room, growing more uneasy by the minute at what was going on. When José finally left them alone, he helped Eva feed the littlest one, who was breathing better after twenty-four hours of oxygen. Enzo saw José outside the window conversing with the men who had brought the incubators. Standing in the middle of the snow, they seemed to be arguing.

'I want to take them to the hospital,' he said.

Eva looked up. She instantly understood how agitated Enzo was.

'They won't be any better anywhere else but here, with him.'

'I don't like owing anyone favours.'

Eva didn't answer right away. She spoke in hushed tones without looking at him, as if it embarrassed her to confess it. She spoke with her eyes fixed on the littler of the two babies. She said she didn't care who he was. She wanted him here, at the side of her two daughters. When José suggested injecting the growth hormone into the weaker of the twins, whose skin was blue from the lack of oxygen, Eva agreed. She had nothing to lose.

* * *

Breeding birds had been one of Enzo's hobbies. He had several failures before succeeding with an initial litter of quails born in a homemade incubator. It was nothing but a wood crate, hermetically sealed, in which he managed to maintain the necessary temperature and humidity during the weeks of gestation. Facing the precarious model of an incubator José's friends had brought, the best they could get on the spur of the moment, Enzo heard the German doctor's instructions. They would need to attach a source of heat, a fan that would circulate the air and a thermostat to control the temperature. In order to compensate for the deficiencies of the respiratory system they were going to regulate the humidity and oxygen levels. If the youngest of the twins got worse, if the oxygenation of her tissues and the brain was insufficient or if she continued to refuse to take nourishment, they would feed her from inside, for which there needed to be a sleeve that would allow one of them, wearing a sterilised glove and using a dropper, to give her, one drop at a time, her mother's milk, enriched with serum, iron and vitamins. If she still couldn't handle that, they would insert a tube. Her defences probably would diminish to an extreme degree or she would suffer some sort of infection and they would need two openings with protection to handle the baby without opening her cubicle.

Enzo made a note of the onslaught of possibilities.

He spent the next twenty-four hours holed up in his shop.

For greater security they had decided to divide the house in two. The left wing was for the sick, which is where they moved Lilith and her younger brother, along with the two guests from Mendoza, who had succumbed to the illness. The right wing was reserved for the mother and the premature babies, along with Tomás and Enzo, who showed no signs of the illness. Luned decided to take care of the ones who were sick and she ordered her stockier cousins to devote themselves full time to the twins.

When the snow stopped, the few healthy guests decided to leave for healthier climes. The light of the house changed, now the blinds were kept closed to keep out the cold; the sounds changed too, laughter and voices in various languages giving way to silence and the crying of the newborns; and its smell, as the Welshwomen decided to scrub the house with bleach, as though that could impede the advance of germs. José was the only one who came and went freely, although he took extreme precautions, putting on a surgical mask before examining the sick and washing his hands in alcohol as soon as he was done. The house was soon transformed into his playground. Not since he'd arrived in Argentina had he had two subjects of study as pure and identical and that, if it weren't for him, would already have death certificates in their name. Although he pretended to be administering the same treatment to both of them in terms of injections, serum, fortified milk and warmth, the older one was being given nothing but placebos. He left the stronger of twins to her fate and made the decision to work with the younger one, determined to demonstrate that medicine could change destiny with even the inevitable. He was the only one who went into Bariloche every day, even though the men of the house had to shovel the entrance road for an hour for each foray to make a path for the car. They did it without complaining as a way of thanking him for what he was doing, as the premature babies began to give signs of improvement.

Especially the weaker one.

José examined her several times a day. The quality of her breathing, her weight progression, her tolerance for nourishment... No infectious episodes had occurred and her white blood cell count was up. By the end of two weeks she weighed as much as her sister, who in turn had begun to show signs of deterioration in her respiratory system. The state of the two twins had switched. He had to put on a surgical mask to keep Eva from seeing his happiness over confirming the final phase. He listened to the tiny body, which kept getting weaker and weaker and said there wasn't much more to be done.

'Why is one getting better and the other not?' Eva asked.

Not even her despair kept her from fighting.

'It's all a matter of fate,' José said.

He suggested she get in bed with the baby and hold her as she said goodbye. He bit his lip on the verge of offering to take charge of the preparations for burial. It was vital not to get ahead of himself. Daily events had become an adventure story which he wrote down in his black notebook with the urgency of a maniac: data, calculations and statistics that even crowded around the margins. The family's small domestic tragedy which he shared had turned him into an addict, providing him with free doses of drama as the twins struggled against death several times a day. He rode this drama with antibiotics, hormones, serum, oxygen and injections with the omnipotence of a god.

The first snowfall around that time brought with it their isolation.

Nahuel Huapi froze over, but the cold snap was so intense that very few adventurous types had the courage to go skating around the edges of the lake. Even though the heaters were lit day and night, they failed to warm the house. Lilith spent a few days in bed, clutching a hot water bottle. If it hadn't been for the state of confusion and delirium brought on by the very high fevers at the outset, Lilith would have begged her parents not to leave her alone with him in the left wing. What had happened in the guesthouse on the outskirts of Trelew was still a part of the realm of her nightmares. The images came to her at night, when her temperature soared and her parents weren't there to hear her cry. Luned was the only one who brought her fever down with cold cloths, convinced that her inexplicable anguish would fade when they had won the battle against pneumonia.

Now that he had her close by, José visited her often.

He took her temperature, listened to her chest and felt her lymph glands as he told her about the microscopic improvement of her sisters. One night José made her lie in warm water for hours so her 104 degree temperature would lower with the temperature of the water. Her stomach was covered with microscopic scars, bundles of puncture points she had received in the past months. The marks on the door of her room told no lies. She had grown a few fractions of an inch in five months. No one stopped to reflect on whether Lilith's condition was to do with the epidemic and the winter cold or instead with the battery of chemicals her body had taken on in the past weeks. When she opened her eyes she saw him sitting in a corner of the bathroom. He was observing the outlines of her body, which was shivering under her shift with a hunger that he already knew by heart.

'Leave me alone.'

'You really want me to leave?'

'Yes.'

It was a plea not an order. The two knew that no one was going to kick out the man who was saving her sisters' lives. She didn't really want him to leave, although the desire for him to remain produced in her something worse than pneumonia. Her feverish and delirious state gave a measure of strangeness to the routine of the injection. Lilith let him raise her shift, as though her body belonged to him and not to her. She liked to see how the syringe entered her flesh.

'How come you haven't assembled them?'

'Who?'

'The dolls.'

'You can't assemble a doll.'

'I said, why don't you assemble their parts?'

'When the twins get better.'

He withdrew the syringe and placed a piece of cotton dipped in alcohol on her vein. Lilith followed each movement as if in slow motion. The German had been repeating the same thing for days, *when the twins get better*. Their premature birth was the perfect excuse to leave the assembly of the dolls hanging.

'You're lying,' Lilith murmured.

But he didn't even bother to answer her. He continued to wash her feverish body with a damp cloth.

'You like them like that,' she insisted, her voice hoarse because of the fever.

He spread her legs to clean her.

It was true. He couldn't overcome the secret delight in keeping them unassembled. The previous afternoon Lilith had gathered the strength to walk down the hallway to José's room. She pushed the door open and stood there looking at them, heads in one bag, arms in another, legs, torsos, everything piled up in front of the mirror and repeated to infinity, with the little blonde wigs piled up on top of the chest of drawers, the bag with the glass eyes sitting on the desk. Even the clothes the Welshwoman had sewn by hand were ready there. She had obediently followed the patterns José had given her, a cloying synthesis of all of the uniforms of the Third Reich.

Nobody seemed to be in any hurry, now that everything was ready, to assemble, dress and offload them. The drama of the twins made them all forget the business venture with the same vehemence with which they planned it.

Lilith walked around the bags, grabbed a pair of the eyes and attached them to one of the heads. The doll suddenly was looking at her, without a body to kick with, without vocal cords to scream. She added trunk, arms, legs. When she was done, she set the little wig on the head. The fever that came on every afternoon sent her into a state of emergency. She dragged the bags stuffed with the members from José's room to her own and stacked them around her bed. When the Frenchman with the cameras knocked on her door to say goodbye, she already had half a dozen dolls assembled, the hairpieces sewn on like José taught her, with the glass buttons inserted in their sockets. Many of them were naked, only half completed. They lacked one or both arms, a leg, the eyes... Some were put together completely. The Frenchman could no longer stand the air of intrigue that surrounded the guesthouse. Before saying good-bye, he hugged her and whispered in her ear.

'If things aren't right, you can say so.'

Lilith nodded but she didn't say a word.

Neither that day nor any other.

She asked him for a photograph of the doll to hang on the school's bulletin board. Someone had to think about sell-ing them. The Frenchman agreed to develop that last photo before leaving. He knew that, sooner or later, it would be proof when he went to the police. His plan was to get far enough away from Bariloche to make a few phone calls. He wasn't the only one who suspected the alliances that were being forged in the city. José understood everything that was going on and his paranoia grew by the day. He saw in the looks exchanged by strangers in the streets enemies prepared to turn him in. He lived with a sensation of vertigo, but he refused to simply vanish into thin air. His colleagues begged him to leave. Everything was in place to whisk him through a border crossing with Chile. Even his neighbour insisted he avoid land routes, and the hydroplane was ready to take him from Patagonia whenever he wanted.

But José always answered with the same phrase.

'Tomorrow.'

He spent his afternoons in a small room in the back of the vet clinic examining the blood samples taken from Enzo's daughters. Eva no longer objected to his taking her blood or that of her daughters and she would have sold her soul for him not to let them die. When the most furious of the snowstorms covered the city and its surroundings with the same blanket of snow, everyone was submerged in an all-enveloping obsession that seemed to entrap them.

Eva had become a worker with a single goal.

José was the boss who gave the orders.

Lilith was his prisoner.

When the flu turned into pneumonia, she understood that she was going to remain in the left wing for an unknown period of time isolated and quarantined. She no longer even asked to see her family. Communication was reduced to a couple of notes exchanged through José, who was the only one to cross the threshold between the healthy and the sick, as though immune to all illness.

12

Nora Edloc arrived in Bariloche the same afternoon they took the weaker of the premature babies out of the incubator. While the plane was taxiing down a snow-covered runway, she asked herself if it was for real this time. She had spent her life looking for him and she had no intention of doing anything else until the day she died. In the bed of a rank-smelling highly placed official, after he had used her body as he wished, as had so many others, she saw one of José's dolls on a bookcase reserved for books on Nazi esoterica, the new religion of many during the decline of the empire. Still naked, she walked around the room with a cigarette hanging from her lips. She took the doll down without asking permission. She knew that the minutes right after sex were the best time to ask questions. And the pig who was still writhing with pleasure in the bed had neither daughters nor granddaughters. She asked him if he was thinking about collecting dolls.

'It's not a doll… It's a trophy.'

Now that they had nothing, they lived off myths. Nora knew them all. She had followed thousands of false leads. She spoke Spanish with a Buenos Aires accent and had an Argentine passport, although Buenos Aires had been her home for only a few years. It wasn't in that encounter but several times later, when the doll was always just one more woman in bed, that the pig finally talked. He said his small plastic trophy was the living proof that the most important minds of medicine were still alive. He didn't know exactly where, but the colleague that had brought it to him was from Bariloche.

The next day Nora was on her way south.

For years she had been chipping away at the little bit left of the family fortune in her search for him. There was no one left but her to spend it, so she spent it without any guilt. She checked into the Hotel Catedral and set about doing the same thing as the other tourists. She rented a pair of skis and went up on the slope three days in a row. Her style was impeccable. She slid along the runs without poles, bending her body right and left in a dance that was a show of grace and precision. She knew that in order to get close to the circles in which they moved she would have to be patient and let them come to her like flies. She also had to spend money, going to the best hotels and restaurants and dressed like a lady. She had to show she was alone, available but alone. She lost no time in seducing this one and that. They were geniuses at climbing casually into the lift that took them back to the top. She was an expert in the art of conversation and could lead them like lambs to the slaughter. But she had to be cautious. Any question out of the ordinary would sound the alarm.

Otto Arko, a Slovene who worked rescue on the mountain, found her skiing off piste an hour before sunset. She glided carefree through the trees on the west side of the slope.

She's as calm as someone about to commit suicide, Arko, who knew something about these things, thought.

It was the calm of a survivor who has been thousands of times in desperate situations. The snow had begun to frost over and the fog was covering the slope like a curtain. He zigzagged over to her and stopped her a few yards downhill.

'Are you lost?' he asked.

'I guess so.'

'I'll lead you. You've got to get off the slope.'

He went on ahead, looking back over his shoulder at each curve to make sure she was still there, a few yards away. He kept looking for more and more demanding shortcuts when he saw how she met each obstacle calmly without a single stumble. Although her face was completely covered by a leather cap, goggles and an angora scarf, Arko surmised that she was a beautiful woman. He confirmed it at the bottom of the slope, when Nora removed the layers of clothes she was wearing and invited him to a whisky as a gesture of gratitude. Arko, who was still on duty, accepted immediately. Tomorrow he'd deal with the suspension he was most certainly going to receive for disappearing during the time when the rescue patrol was most in demand, especially on foggy days when the mountain was covered with lost skiers. Any mortal would understand how difficult it was to resist such an offer. Nora asked him if he had a car to go the ten miles that separated the base camp from the ski centre in Bariloche. Her hotel was one of the few constructions at the top, the most opulent of all, but she didn't tell him she was staying at El Catedral. She checked her skis and followed him out to an old Volkswagen.

She was quiet on the road into town, watching the countryside through the window. Her distracted manner always drove the men wild. Arko knew instantly that she was one of those women for whom commitment is a dirty word. The possibility of walking the same streets as the man of her nightmares kept her awake at night and she spent long hours in the hotel bar. The Slovene, who was much more sensitive than Nora guessed, also realised something else. No matter how strong she seemed to be, she was a broken woman. She had dark circles under her eyes that not even make-up could disguise and a slight tremor in her left hand. Her drinking was accompanied by the rage she felt over how the man she had been seeking for more than a decade might be living a peaceful life in a paradise such as the one she saw from the hotel's huge picture windows. When the third drink had gone to his head, Arko could no longer hold back the desire to ask the question.

'Do you plan on staying here long?'

'Two weeks.'

'Are you here alone?'

Nora looked him in the eye and smiled, barely, before answering.

'Actually, I have a German friend I've lost touch with. I know he lives here in Bariloche.'

She asked herself if the man she had been trying to find for two decades would recognise her when they were face to face again. She knew she should have no illusions. She had already followed dozens of false leads.

'May I ask you a question, Otto?'

She bit down on a piece of ice that burst into bits on her tongue. The people from Mossad would need to assemble a mechanism to extradite him. She, on the other hand, only needed one night alone with him.

'How many times have you rescued people who'd been going in circles in the middle of a snow storm?'

'Hundreds.'

'And at the moment they saw you, what could you see in their eyes… Resignation or struggle?'

'Do you really want to know?'

Nora nodded.

'People who die on the mountain always have their eyes open. The end sneaks up on them. That's how the cold is. It gets in your bones. It kills when you think you can still go on.'

Nora opened her mouth to respond, but Arko stopped her with a gesture of his hand.

'Now it's my turn.'

'Ask away.'

'How come a woman like you only talks of death?'

Her answer would have turned everything into a child's game. She only smiled.

'Is there anything more interesting?'

The jolt of oxygen cleared her head as they went out to the street.

The first tiny flakes of snow were just starting to fall.

At the end of the block she stopped to look at some puppies in the door of a vet clinic. Her clothes were slightly uncomfortable and dizziness made her lean against the window. She would never have guessed that a few yards away in the back room of the clinic the man she was looking for was studying some blood samples from the twins. Seeing her looking faint, Arko held Nora by the waist... Her lips and fingernails were blue.

'Are you all right?'

'I had a drop in blood pressure.'

'I'll take you to your hotel,' he suddenly said, speaking to her more intimately.

Nora didn't answer. For a moment he thought it was the alcohol that made her head towards the corner, but he stopped when he saw her enter the Bariloche Deutsche Schule with the precision of an arrow. She was so quick that Arko had to run the last few yards to catch up with her. He found her standing in the middle of the lobby. Her head was slightly turned up and her nostrils were tense. She always combated inebriation with the same tactic, reaching for a glimmer of serenity in her disturbed and furious state.

'If you're looking for a German, this is the place to find him.'

Nora didn't bother to tell him he was mistaken. No one was going to give her the answers she was seeking. She knew that Primo Capraro had been closed during the war. Two years before, the German community had opened the doors of a new institution, although as a precaution the name of the school and the building were different. She walked through the halls looking at the photographs hanging from the walls. The images from the past had been carefully chosen. The flags touted no swastikas and there were no Nazi insignia or salutes. Various similar institutions in different cities of the world operated with the same pact of silence. You had to belong to very intimate circles to reach certain citizens. Yet rumors still got out. Nora knew them by heart. Hitler's birthday was always celebrated every April in a centrally located guesthouse. Nazi meetings were held twice a month in the hideouts in Cerro López. There were several members of the SS on the board of Primo Capraro College…

A hand-coloured photograph in the middle of a bulletin board crowded with information made her stop. The blonde angel with glass eyes and plastic features that looked out at her with the smile of an orphan girl was identical to the pig's doll that had brought her to the south. Both of them had that furious and hallucinated look. There was a telephone number with a local prefix: EUROPEAN-STYLE DOLLS.

Seconds later the doors of the classrooms opened and the hallways filled with children. Many were speaking German. They weren't the majority, but they were the only ones Nora heard. Like an orchestra conductor, she proceeded to silence those who spoke Spanish until she could no longer hear them at all. German would forever be for her the language of horror and hearing it there produced a sinister effect on her. When she turned her head, she saw Arko standing next to her. Still wearing their ski clothes, with their eyes bleary from alcohol and with the vertigo of the mountainside stamped on their faces, they looked as foreign as two space aliens. She sensed the effect their presence must have produced among the students, who began to gather around them.

'We should leave,' she managed to say.

But it was too late. A teacher came up to them. Over her shoulder Nora saw another one coming over. The hour to act had arrived. It would be neither the first nor the last. Her life, after all, was one big simulation.

'Don't say a thing,' she whispered to Arko. 'Leave it to me.'

She smiled with the calm of a professional. She explained that she was thinking of moving to Bariloche the following year with her husband and their children. They were scouting both a house and a school. The youngest, a girl, was seven and couldn't wait to move to Patagonia. The oldest, a ten-year-old boy, had agreed to move under the condition they let him choose the school. With an innocence so genuine that it left Arko wide-eyed, she asked if the school accepted children who were not German. She knew that German education was synonymous with excellence. Yes, of course, she would like to see the facilities. But when she came back, when her family was with her. No, she said with a laugh, and her laughter was the height of warmth, the Slovene was not her husband… He was her guide. The preceptor whispered something in the teacher's ear, who immediately recognised the man with the rescue patrol who more than once had saved one of the students who'd become lost on the slope. Arko could have sworn that the stranger who was reinventing herself before his eyes was glassy-eyed as she described her family's enthusiasm over the move. Without a doubt, what she had said during the past few minutes was the truth. The solitary individual who invented the two hours they'd spent drinking was pure fiction. Before saying goodbye, Nora looked again at the blonde angel who smiled down at her from the photograph.

'Do you know where I can find one of those dolls?'

'The father of one of our children makes them.'

'I'd like to take one as a gift to my little girl.'

'If you have a moment, I'll introduce you,' the teacher said.

She turned to ask the preceptor in German, 'Which grade is having its photograph taken?'

'First year.'

The teacher nodded. It seemed natural to her that the woman would not want to leave Bariloche without one of those dolls. For some strange reason, a mixture of snobbism and chance, it had begun to be a symbol of acceptance to have one. She herself had ordered one from Enzo.

'Do you have a moment just now?'

'All the time in the world,' Nora answered with a glacial smile. 'I'm on vacation.'

She followed her to the courtyard, where some thirty children waited their turn for the annual picture. Two teachers were arranging Lilith's group in symmetrical rows, with the shortest in front, while a photographer was finishing setting up his camera on a tripod. One of the little girls held a chalkboard on which Nora read:

Capraro Elementary School
1960

The photographer took two pictures before signalling to the preceptor that he was ready for the individual photographs. He set up a camera under a tree in a corner of the courtyard, while a preceptor sent the children over one at a time, beginning with the youngest. The teacher pointed out a little girl to Nora. She looked tiny and fragile and she walked toward the photographer slowly, as if each step were an effort.

'She's the daughter of the man who makes the dolls,' she said.

The preceptor went over to the girl and said something that made her turn toward the smiling stranger dressed in ski clothes. Seconds later she walked toward her, trying to hide her enthusiasm.

'The lady would like to buy one of your dad's dolls.'

Nora studied her point blank. She was pale with rings under her eyes. Even when she smiled there seemed to be something dark in her face. She convinced herself that she was the one to see shadows even in children.

'Do you people make them?'

'At home,' Lilith said.

'And you sell them here?'

'For the time being.'

'Her family has a guesthouse in the Belgrano neighbourhood. If you'd like to see them, I'm sure Arko could take you there…'

'Of course.'

'Is your father home, Lilith?'

'He always is.'

'Then go now. Leave your bicycle in the shed.'

'I didn't come by bicycle.'

After several weeks being cooped up they had finally allowed her to return to school. If she didn't suffer a relapse they were going to move her back to the right wing of the house where she could get acquainted with her sisters. For the time being she saw them from a distance. Although she had lived only a few yards from her family, she felt like she'd been sent into exile in a faraway land, one in which José was king. The world had changed for her after that first night during the trip to Trelew. Her laughter was no longer a flood of joy and it was no longer necessary to tell her to keep quiet and stop inventing fantasy worlds. But everything had been camouflaged by the illness and no one knew that Lilith was a different person. Eva was convinced that the traces of pneumonia in her blood were what made her listless and silent.

A block from the school, Lilith asked Arko to stop the car in front of the door of the vet clinic. She jumped out of the car and ran to the door of the clinic. She banged on the door with her left fist first, then with her right one and five seconds later with both. Days before the owner of the vet clinic had received the order to keep the door of his business shut whenever José was working in the back and to not let anyone in he didn't know. He closed the door behind Lilith and stood there looking at the two strangers waiting in the car. In the front seat Arko looked at Nora out of the corner of his eye.

'When are you moving?'

'Who?'

'Your family.'

'What family?'

Nora never wondered why she choked up whenever she invented lives for herself in which she was not alone. At times she fantasised about giving up, but then pursued the next clue when she realised she had no place to go home to.

'I don't have any children nor do I have a husband. I don't even have a pet,' Nora said, her eyes fixed on the door of the vet clinic. 'Everything I own can fit into a suitcase. And I could get rid of it without the slightest problem.'

'And what you said back there?'

'Don't believe anything I say, Arko.'

'Nothing,' the Slovene whispered, calling out to her.

She must have heard his plea because she turned her head to look at him, with a trace of scorn and without pity.

'They're all lies.'

Arko heard her outburst of sincerity with a smile. He'd always had a special attraction to those who told uncomfortable truths and he could have sworn that the description of the two imaginary children couldn't be anything other than the truth, but it was the only real yearning that captivated him about the stranger. He wasn't wrong. Nora's nostalgia for the family she was never going to have was so great that the Slovene had to open the window to breathe.

Lilith found José in the small room in back seated at his worktable. He was preparing a concentrate of mother's milk mixed with serum, iron, hormones and vitamins. The mother's milk, once it was treated, turned into a thicker broth. José placed it in a vial labelled with the name *Alicia*. He set it in a small box with dry ice in which there was another vial that had already been labelled with the name *Berta*.

'Tell your mother we're going to be giving Alicia twelve centimetres starting today. Berta will still get eight.'

Lilith nodded as she undid the two buttons of her top at the level of her belly button. José undid another button without even asking her permission and swiped a cotton pad dipped in alcohol over her skin.

'You're going to have to learn to inject it on your own,' he said in German.

It had been days since he stopped speaking Spanish to her, knowing she understood his language. Lilith felt the prick, barely blinking, as though used to the ritual.

'The christening is today,' she said on her way out. 'Don't be late.'

Outside, the snowflakes were getting thicker and had begun to dust the streets white. Lilith got into the car, which immediately pulled away. Nora's gaze crossed more than once with Lilith's in the rearview mirror. She saw her repeatedly scratching her belly with her hand. Her other hand held the labelled vials on ice which she rested on her legs. On a straight stretch of the road that followed along Nahuel Huapi, Nora couldn't stand the mystery any longer.

'What's that?'

'Milk. For my sisters.'

She scratched her belly again as she spoke.

'Momma removes it every day and José prepares it.'

'Who's José?'

'A vet who lives with us.'

Nora felt a lump in her throat.

Of course, it would be just like him to use his own name, she thought.

She knew the endless list of false identities by heart: Friedrich Edler Von Breitenbach, Gregorio Grigori, Helmut Gregor, Karl Geuske, Alfredo Mayen, Fritz Fischer, Walter Hasek, Fausto Rindón, Enrique Wollman, José Aspiazi, Lars Ballestroen, Juan Lechin, Ernst Sebastián Alvez... But why not use his real name? Argentina had awarded amnesty to everyone who had immigrated with false names. Dozens of colleagues had reclaimed their original names. And no one was looking for him until a few months ago.

She turned to look at the vials of milk.

'Are they twins?' she asked.

'Identical twins, born prematurely.'

'Are they doing better?'

'The littler one is growing faster than her sister.'

Lilith scratched herself again. The itching was sometimes unbearable.

'Does it hurt you?'

'It itches. What hurts me are my bones. But it's a good sign.'

'Hurting is never a good sign,' Nora said.

She didn't ask her what signs she meant, but she was beginning to get an idea. She couldn't stop thinking she was about the same age when she met him. That's what she thought, that they were about the same size. Lilith was already going on thirteen and José had begun to play with Nora's body much before that.

She kept her suspicions to herself, studying the house in the Belgrano neighbourhood she could see behind rows of pines. She knew that for years no one had bothered to ask any questions when a new immigrant had arrived to take up residence in the city. On the contrary, they received them with open arms. They would lower the prices of the houses for sale, finding them jobs and arranging documents. They would make them members of their clubs and invite them to their parties, refraining from asking what they were escaping from unless they happened to be in the most intimate circles.

Arko stopped the car in front of the door of the guesthouse.

Something told Arko he wasn't going to see her again, but still he took a chance and asked, 'Should I wait?'

'It won't be necessary.'

Nora got out of the car and followed Lilith down a dirt road lined with pine trees. She didn't even turn around to wave to him. Arko had the feeling that it wasn't just alcohol that made her walk like that. He would have liked to shake her and tell her that there was still time for her to have a life. He could not imagine then that two days later he would find her under the snow, in a crevice in the mountain, with her eyes open.

13

There were already a dozen cars at the end of the road lined with trees when they got there, parked between two small mounds of snow that Tomás had shovelled for an hour to make room for the invited guests. A thick fog began to weave itself among the houses and trees surrounding the lake, engulfing them. Lilith stopped when she saw Cumín seated behind the wheel of an old pick-up, with the motor running and the lights on. She confirmed it was him when she saw Yanka appear from behind the curtain of snow that was getting thicker by the minute. She had never forgotten when they exchanged dolls or the surprise over seeing a girl her age pregnant. Now, instead of her belly, Yanka was holding Herlitzka by the neck.

'What are you doing here?' Lilith asked.

'You've got something that belongs to us.'

'I don't understand…'

'Wakolda.'

'We traded.'

'You've got to return her to me,' Yanka said, fear in her voice.

If she were still alive it was because she had given birth only days before Cumín had discovered Herlitzka buried underneath his bed. They had spent months tracking the family down, remembering only that the family had been travelling south. But Patagonia was too vast for that bit of information to be enough. For a brief moment Lilith thought it was all part of her nightmares. The blonde dolls had taken over every corner of the room that was her bunker during the epidemic.

The ones that had turned out the best slept on the nightstand, while the others filled the shelves. One night, opening her eyes in the middle of the dark, she saw all the little heads turned toward her. She would have sworn that some of them were missing an arm or a leg.

They've torn pieces from themselves, she thought.

She knew that the ones that were done went away and they didn't want to leave her. She convinced herself that it was the dolls and not her who were lacking peace. Yesterday, when she began to gather her things to move back to the other side of the house, she realised that something of herself was going to stay behind forever in that room. A piece had already been torn from her. Enzo agreed to leave the dolls in José's room, lined up one beside the other. The German had convinced him that there was no need to get a place in the city.

'The more secret they are, the better,' he said.

The only doll that didn't scare Lilith, who felt more mixed blood than ever among so much Aryan purity, was Wakolda. She hugged her so tight one night she felt something in her belly. Disoriented by the fever, she told José that the Mapuche doll had something hidden inside her… She was pregnant, just like her first owner. She made him rest his hand on the swollen and ragged cloth.

'Don't you feel it?' she whispered.

The German must have felt something, because in the morning Wakolda's stomach had been poorly stitched back together. Lilith frowned as she looked at the stitches…

'What did you do to her?' she asked the German doctor when he came by to see her.

José just smiled.

He dried her forehead with a damp cloth and whispered in her ear, 'Your friend has no idea what she gave you.'

192

Yes… They do, Lilith thought as she walked back to the house. She promised to go find it and return.

'We're going to go fetch it ourselves if you don't bring it,' Yanka said.

And she let her go.

Curiosity to see if the famous dolls were as perfect as they were rumoured to be had drawn some fifty people from their homes in the middle of a snowstorm to be present at the christening of the twins. Through the windows, Nora saw a group of people gathered around a preaching priest who was holding one of the twins in his hands. Eva was standing next to him, happy in spite of her exhaustion. She held the weaker of her daughters in her arms, ready to be blessed. None of those present could imagine the fight that child had put up to stay alive. Nora was intrigued as she looked at Lilith. She was in no hurry at all to go inside, even though the ceremony was almost over.

'Shouldn't you at least be there?'

'They won't let me.'

'They won't let you in your own house?'

Lilith shrugged her shoulders with the resignation of an adult. Her months of quarantine had made her used to watching life through the window.

'I had pneumonia… They won't let me near my sisters.'

'For how long?'

'Not until they're convinced I'm all cured.'

She still had some congestion that made those standing near her back away when she had a fit of coughing. Far from bothering her, it worked like an invisible shield, and if she wanted someone to keep his distance all she had to do was to shower him with her germs.

'Have you been baptised?' Lilith asked.

193

Nora didn't think it was either the moment or the place to explain her relationship with God after having been brought up in a concentration camp.

'No.'

'Me neither.'

'Why haven't you, if they are?'

'My parents where atheists when I was little.'

'And now?'

'Now I'm the one who doesn't want to.'

Nora smiled at her. Her little hostess' rage reminded her of how she had been at the same age. Inside, the priest placed the twins in the holy water. The weaker of the two whimpered more softly than her sister because her lungs were still weak. There was no doubt in Lilith's mind. What was going on there was a miracle that had nothing to do with God. Nora wasn't in any hurry to go inside either. She examined the face of each one of the guests, wondering if she would recognise him beneath so many beards and moustaches.

The lights of the Chevrolet outlined the two of them.

It wasn't even five o'clock but the sky, overcast and grey from the snow, had turned dark in the course of the last hour. Lilith recognised José's car before he'd turned off the lights and engine. She had no idea that the stranger who walked alongside him with unsure footsteps had had her own child-hood destroyed by the same man when she was the same age. Seconds later she saw him slash the white blanket that surrounded them with his black suit and hat.

'There he is,' she said.

Nora knew it was him two hundred yards away.

She hadn't realised she remembered so many details. He was as impeccably dressed as always, with his aristocratic gait and that strange mixture of condescension and morbid ferocity that came from years of deciding who would live and who would die. She had imagined thousands of times what meeting him again would be like and in her fantasies the meeting was never like this, trivial and rapid without any preamble. Now that she was finally face to face with him, all she could feel was terror.

'Have they already started?' he asked without saying hello.

'It's over,' Lilith replied.

José opened the front door and let them in.

He took his hat and overcoat off in the hall. He had done nothing to change his appearance. He used neither beard nor moustache, nor had he been operated on like so many others. He hadn't even aged. She could barely look at him, barely conceal the trembling of her hand when Lilith introduced them. José had not stopped to look at her, but he could sense that the woman was on the verge of panic.

'Are you just passing through?' he asked, although he already knew the answer.

'She wants to buy a doll,' Lilith said.

'May I ask who it's for?'

'My daughter,' Nora said.

The one I would have had if I'd never met you, she thought.

José took a few minutes to answer, as though listening to each one of her thoughts. There was no doubt he knew her. He took some keys form his pocket and gave them to Lilith.

'Can you show them to her?'

He nodded to Nora.

'Excuse me.'

Although he could not recognise the little girl hidden in this woman's past, he knew that one of the many fortune hunters that combed Argentina looking for him had finally found him.

And she wasn't alone.

When he came out of the vet clinic, a Ford that was parked on the corner caught his attention. The fog kept him from seeing how many people were inside. But he knew immediately who they were and what they were looking for. At a bend in the road, a few miles from Bariloche, a Ford pulled out from a crossroads and began to follow his car at a discreet distance.

José made no attempt to get away.

It had been snowing in the afternoon for days. The wind came up with the snow and the effect was a thick white cloud that made cars travel in slow motion, with their foglights on as well as their normal ones. It would be suicidal to step on it on a mountain road covered in snow and he had a much quicker and cleaner method. He took the pill from his pocket and closed it in the palm of his hand.

He thought, *whoever said it wasn't going to end this way?*

The Ford began to draw closer, like a shark preparing to attack.

Why would it be better to die an old man?

They followed him to the door of the guesthouse, but did not enter through the gate. José saw in the rearview mirror that the car stopped at the edge of the property.

Just for the pleasure of having made a fool out of all of them, he answered himself. *Because the best crime of all is the one that goes unpunished.*

He knew it was just a matter of minutes.

He turned the engine off and sat there quietly, listening for a few moments to the silence of the mountain. He prepared his Colt and got out of the car. They probably had a number of cars patrolling the area. His head clear with the hunt that was about to begin, he walked toward the house. He knew when he'd said hello to Nora they were waiting for confirmation of his identity before coming in to get him. The moment had come to disappear into thin air, but he was going to do it his way, with complete attention to detail.

Once inside the house, José made his way among the people flashing smiles and shaking hands. He'd long ceased to be an outsider. He had been accepted by everyone, those who knew who he was, those who suspected it and those who lived a blind existence without guilt. He paused to say something to two men, who immediately left the room. In no hurry, he took a handful of candy from his pocket and distributed it among a group of children who came running. Even the priest made space for him at his side before blessing the twins whom God and medicine had saved from death. Nora struggled to hold back a rush of forgotten memories, all traumatic and buried...

She recalled how the youngest ones had called him *Uncle Pepi*.

He brought them sweets and toys and then personally led them to the gas chambers. It had been years since she'd thought about Ina and Guido, Romanian twins. He sewed them back to back, wanting to create Siamese twins. The wounds became infected. One night they cried in pain for hours, until their mother stole some morphine and killed them to keep them from suffering any longer.

'Let us pray,' the priest said.

The guests all stood up around him.

José bowed his head and closed his eyes.

The image of the two baby girls submerged in water before José was too much for Nora, who could barely stop herself from retching. She felt Lilith's hand in hers. She followed her to the side of the house reserved for guests. For years she had speculated about what she was going to do when she met him. The only variable she hadn't taken into account was that she would be unable to control her emotions. Or that the flash-backs would place her once again in the experiment room, naked among so many other adolescents who waited their turn as guinea pigs to be infected with malaria, jaundice and typhus, or to be used for freezing, infection of wounds, gangrene, tetanus, amputations, poisonings, burns…

Lilith stopped in front of a closed door.

There were the numerous marks that had been made on the frame by José's dagger.

'What's this?' Nora asked, although she already had an idea.

'My height.'

Lilith pointed to the first one.

'That's me a couple of months ago…'

Inside, the Aryan dolls were arranged along all the shelves. The room had been transformed into a sanctuary. Nora walked around without touching a thing. She examined the bed where José had slept during the last months, with a view of Nahuel Huapi.

'How long ago did you open the guesthouse?'

'During the summer. José was the first… He says he brought us luck.'

Lilith picked up one of the dolls and moved the lever in its neck so it would follow Nora with its glass eyes.

'There's a lever her in back… See?'

The doll looked at Nora without expression.

'Take your pick.'

'They scare me a bit.'

'They scare you? Why, they're only babies…'

'They don't have the eyes of babies. No baby looks like that.'

'What do you mean?'

'Like you.'

Before she ended up in José's hands, Nora had fainted every time she saw blood. She had no tolerance for pain. Her older brother always used to tell her that you had to be strong to face the world. In the end, he resisted less than she did.

'I used to look the same way at your age.'

She saw some clothes hanging in the closet, shirts, a suit, and suitcase... That's why he never left a trace, travelling almost with only the clothes on his back. She stopped in front of three dolls that were on a shelf separated from the rest, with little dresses inspired by the uniforms of the Third Reich. One of them had a particularly crafty shine in its pupils and two perfect braids.

'I'll take this one,' she said, picking it up.

'Those are the most expensive ones. Their clothes are tailor-made and the hair is real. I'm not even sure if those are for sale...'

'Ask him,' Nora said, as she drew a Minox camera from her handbag. 'May I?'

Without waiting for a reply, she took a couple of pictures of the dolls and the room. When she turned around she saw that Lilith was watching her from the door, serious, with the look of an adult.

'You've got to come with me,' she said.

She locked the door before leading her back to the living room. The party was in full swing. Someone had put on some music and a few courageous people were already dancing, urging the shyer ones to join in. Nora knew what she had to do. She had seen a phone in the office that opened out onto the entrance hall. She saw José talking to Lilith to one side in a corner. Seconds later the German doctor made his way toward Nora with two glasses of champagne in his hands.

'Please,' he said, smiling like a gentleman.

'No, I shouldn't… I've got to drive to my hotel.'

'I'm sure there's someone who can take you. There's never any lack of solidarity in this place… And this is a night to celebrate.'

Nora had no choice but to accept.

'Let's go,' the German said.

Without waiting for an answer, he grabbed her around the waist to take her to the dance floor.

'You chose one of my favourite dolls.'

He had to talk into her ear so she could hear him above the music. The contact of her skin with José's overwhelmed her with a host of emotions. Enveloped by the fear of loathing, fear and rage, she recognised the same excitement he had produced in her the first nights they spent together.

'Do you know their hair is real?'

'I didn't touch them,' Nora said.

He drew her body closer, his open palm placed just above Nora's tailbone.

'So you like to take pictures…'

Nora took a sip of champagne.

'I'm a photographer,' she said, attempting a smile. 'In addition to being a tourist.'

'And what kind of photography do you do?'

'A bit of everything.'

'Forensic photography?'

'Excuse me?'

'Have you ever photographed dead bodies?'

For an instant, Nora looked at him in silence.

'Once. In Ushuaia. Five mountain climbers who got lost on a mountain…'

'Tell me about it, Eldoc…'

'Nora.'

'I like Eldoc better.'

'Then I should also address you by your last name.'

José smiled. Their conversation was already an open duel.

'Do you think a person can sense he's living the last hours of his life?'

'Do you plan on dying soon?'

'Not yet… I have a couple of things to do first.'

'Then that's the strangest question someone I've just met has ever asked me.'

'It's one of those obsessions I have…'

José drew a little closer still, as though it were a confession.

'…every time I see the photograph of someone who has died.'

'How's that?'

'If in the instant he pulls the trigger…'

'My camera is not a weapon.'

José smiled as he gave her a twirl.

'But I imagine those mountain climbers fought to the end, even when it was helpless…'

Nora attempted to set her glass down, put she missed the mark. The glass fell to the ground and broke into pieces, splashing various dancers around them.

'Don't worry about it,' José said amused.

She continued to look into his eyes, unfazed by how others were looking at her.

'No one knows he's living his final hours, unless justice or illness has condemned him…'

José looked at her for a few more seconds, in no hurry.

He smiled and moved to leave.

'I'll go get your doll, Nora.'

Convinced the German doctor was living his final moments of freedom, Nora stopped one of the Welshwomen on her way out of the kitchen with a tray filled with glasses of champagne. She knew what she had to do. She had to ask for a telephone, place the call they had been waiting decades for and confirm the identity of the man who had sterilised her fifteen years ago.

14

José grabbed his suitcase, overcoat and hat he'd left in the entrance hall and walked down the passage that connected the right wing with the left. Lilith was the only one to follow him, as quietly as a shadow. No one remained upstairs. The silence made each creak of the wooden floor echo against the walls. She pushed open the door of her room and found him packing a few things in his suitcase. Only the most necessary things: the note-book, papers, some books… She knew there was little time left.

'I need to ask you a favour,' the German said.

Lilith parted the lace curtain over the window facing the gate and looked out. Through the snowdrifts and the fog, she managed to see the pickup where Cumín and his children were waiting.

'Some men are going to come for me.'

'When?'

'Now, in a few minutes.'

José grabbed one of the Aryan dolls and set it on the pillow.

'Bring them here.'

'Why?'

'Because I asked you to.'

'So what?' Lilith asked.

She was furious because she saw he was leaving forever. José lifted her chin with the tip of his fingers and made her look him in the eye.

'And you'd do anything I asked you to.'

'No.'

'Really?'

Lilith yanked herself away.

'No...' she repeated.

'...please don't leave,' Nora begged Eva at the same moment in the office downstairs.

She still held the phone in her hand.

Seconds before, Eva had overheard her speak a few words in Hebrew to someone on the other end of the line. She backed away, less as a reflex at overhearing someone else's conversation than out of fear. She closed the door and stood waiting for the stranger. She put the blanket she used to wrap around her daughters on the desk and placed the child down on top. She proceeded for a few moments to change her nappy in silence. Nora suspected that the owner of the house expected her to apologise for being at her daughters' christening without having been invited and for having wandered around until she found a telephone, using it without permission. She was wrong. With her gaze fixed on her child, Eva was debating whether or not to ask about what she had sensed months ago.

'Who?' she finally asked, looking at her.

'My name is Nora Edloc and I've come to...'

'The man who lives with us,' Eva interrupted her.

'Do you really want to know?'

Eva nodded.

Two days later Nora would not come back from an outing on the piste. Her mangled body would be found in a crevice in the mountains, near a branch of the López riverbed. The embassy would deny she was an Israeli agent, even though she carried a diplomatic passport. According to her death certificate, she died on 12 July 1960 from multiple wounds.

Lilith knew what was going to happen as soon as she saw him leave his room carrying his suitcase and the smaller suitcase in which he always carried his notebook, the blood samples from her family and the growth hormones he had been giving them. She knew she should tell someone, but she didn't. She left by the side door that led out to the back garden and ran until she came face to face with the car in which Cumín and his sons were waiting.

The lights of the pickup were on, shining on her.

She was breathing through her mouth to catch her breath.

She held her hand up to show Wakolda, ready for the exchange of hostages. A few seconds later Yanka got out of the car and walked toward her. She held Herlitzka by the neck.

'You said she had powers,' Lilith said by way of greeting, 'and that she would make my wishes come true.'

'Give her to me.'

'She didn't make a single wish come true.'

'I lied to you.'

'What was she carrying inside?'

The verb in the past tense set off the first alarm bell.

That's when Yanka looked at Wakolda and saw where her cloth body had been sewn shut. She grabbed the doll from her hands and tore her open. A handful of turquoise glass eyes spilled out on the snow. The image was so violent that Lilith leaned down to pick Wakolda up, covered in snow, her belly empty. Yanka turned toward the truck. Immediately Lemún and Nahuel got out of the car.

'Where is he?' Yanka asked.

Lilith didn't answer.

The motor of the hydroplane made her turn around and run off in the direction of the lake. Yanka and her brothers were hard on her heels and would have caught her if Lilith hadn't known the terrain by heart. She dodged every branch, trunk and every stone, counting the seconds until lift off. By contrast, the thorns along the way tore pieces from Wakolda. By the time they reached the lake, she was missing an arm and she was all tattered. At the end of the dock, Lilith went down on her knees to keep from flying into the water. Cumín's sons stopped a few yards away, breathing as hard as she was. They looked up to see the hydroplane emerge from the house next door.

She knew he was looking at her at that moment.

And that he was smiling.

Before leaving he had arranged the doll with the crafty eyes on the bed where he had slept for seven months.

'Leave it there. Don't let anyone touch it.'

It wouldn't be the first he had given away. Several had been sent off to Buenos Aires, Córdoba and Santa Fe. There was even an order from Paraguay. They wrapped them in tissue paper in the dining room of the guesthouse. The first dozen of the Aryan dolls didn't end up in the hands of little girls. They were secret symbols of the resistance in exile.

'Tell them I left it as a gift.'

He stood Lilith against the doorframe. He used the dagger to make the last mark for her height, various inches above the first one.

'We could say you're my work,' he said.

He stood there, looking at her for the last time… She was clutching Wakolda, devastated. He smiled incredulously. In spite of everything his little circus animal loved him.

'You'll forget me.'

The small plane swooped up in flight 300 feet from the coast, flew through a storm and disappeared. Lilith imagined that José was on the other side in a blue sky. '*Love is an act that needs an accomplice*,' he had told her before reaching the Führer's Patagonian bunker. She didn't understand the sentence until

years later. But she never forgot it either. Some day the certainty of having been his accomplice would come to torture her much more than her other secrets.

Biographical Note

Lucía Puenzo, born in 1976, earned her degree in Literature at the University of Buenos Aires and studied at the National Film Institute (INCAA). She is a scriptwriter for film and TV who has written feature films, documentary films and mini-series. For XXY, she was awarded the Grand Prix de la Semaine de la Critique at Cannes Film Festival in 2007, along with three other prizes. Her second film, based on her novel *El Niño Pez*, opened the Panorama Section at the Berlinale Filmfestival 2009. In 2010, Lucía Puenzo was selected for the first-ever issue Best of Young Spanish-Language Novelists of the prestigious English literary magazine *Granta*. Her novel *The German Doctor* has been published in more than ten countries so far. The film, bearing the same title, was presented at the Cannes and San Sebastián Film Festivals and has been released in several countries.